# CURSE of the SORCERER'S BONES

by

## Avraham Shira

PITSPOPANY

NEW YORK ◇ JERUSALEM

Curse of the Sorcerer's Bones
Text copyright © 1995 by Avraham Shira
Illustrations copyright © 1995 by Lisa Perel

ISBN: 0-943706-57-2

Published by PITSPOPANY PRESS

Printed in Hungary

*Special thanks to Yaacov Peterseil*
*and Rabbi Nachman Kahana*
*for their support and creative insights.*

# CURSE of the SORCERER'S BONES

## Chapter 1

# A Secret Revealed

On the kitchen table lay an unopened envelope. Eli picked it up. When he saw his name and the postmark *Israel* he ripped it open and began to read.

*My dear Grandson*, the letter began. But Eli had no grandfather. His parents had lost their parents before he was born.

*I am writing with the hope of seeing you before I die. There is something very valuable here destined for you that was left behind in the Holy Land.*

Something valuable he left behind? But he had never been to Israel, never even left the United States.

*These long years I have waited for you to reach Bar Mitzvah. You are the last of our line. You must be prepared to receive your inheritance. There will be many tests. It will not be easy. You must know there is an evil within and an evil without. But I can teach you to overcome the power of the Other Side.*

Was this some madman's joke? He checked the envelope again. Yes, it was addressed to him. Then he read the closing words.

*I await your arrival.*

*The blessings of Israel be upon you.*

*Saba.*

Eli stared at the letter. Saba? Grandfather? He had a grandfather in Israel? How could that be? Just then Eli heard a car pull into the driveway. The doors slammed and footsteps hurried up the walk.

"Maybe he didn't get home yet," said his mother, as she followed Eli's father into the house.

"I think I left it on the kitchen table," his father said as they came through the doorway from the living room.

Eli was sitting motionless over the letter.

"I don't get it," he said, looking up at them. "How can I have a grandfather in Israel? Didn't you tell me your parents died when I was a little kid?"

His father and mother seemed frozen in time. Eli wondered why his parents looked almost...embarrassed, as though he had caught them in a terrible lie.

"We have something very important to tell you," his mother announced, moving closer to him.

They all sat down at the table and were silent a few moments.

Eli's father finally began, "I once told you, Eli, how difficult it was for your mother and me to have a child. We went to doctors and rabbis for help. We tried everything. But nothing, neither modern medicine nor their blessings worked. Then we heard of a great rabbi, a kabbalist, someone who was revered as a worker of wonders. A mystic. He lived in Jerusalem.

"When all else failed, we went to see him."

Eli had read about kabbalists and the wonders they could do. His teachers at the Jewish Academy had told him stories of some of these great healers and miracle men. Sometimes, in his daydreams, he even imagined himself a great mystic, curing people and changing the world with the power of his mind.

"The kabbalist took us into his room," his father continued. "He had a strange, faraway look in his eyes. Gives me a chill just thinking about it."

Eli saw his father's hand tremble a little.

"Anyway, the rabbi took my hand and gave us a blessing. He said things we didn't understand. Things like God performs many great miracles in this world but we need to open our eyes to see them. And that the joy of one person can be the grief of another, but both joy and grief have one source. Then suddenly, as if he had just received a message from heaven, he told us we would have our baby very soon."

Now it was Eli's turn not to understand. Why were they telling him all this now? He had known for quite some time that a mystic had helped his mother conceive him — within a year after receiving the blessing he had been born. And his mother was never able to have any more children.

"I know I've told you all of this in one form or another," his father said, reading his mind. "But there's a part I never told you. I think you should hear it now."

Harry Bloome looked at his wife. She squeezed his

hand, offering silent encouragement.

"Three weeks later," his father continued, "we were winding our way up a dark mountain road in the Galilee. Suddenly we heard an explosion. A car came swerving around a turn, side-swiped us, and crashed through the guardrail. Miraculously, our right front wheel fell into a ditch at the edge of the road. The impact broke our front axle but saved our lives. The other car...wasn't so lucky. It crashed down the side of the mountain, flipped over, and came to a screeching halt in a ravine. The smell of gasoline was everywhere."

"Your father was very brave," his mother said, looking warmly at her husband. "After he saw that I was all right he climbed down the mountain to help."

Eli's father stared at a spot on the kitchen wall as if he was seeing the accident at that very moment. He spoke slowly, and with difficulty. "Just as I got near the car, flames shot out from under the hood. I yelled at the couple in the front seat to get out, but they were either dead or unconscious. Then I heard a baby crying. I smashed the back window with a rock, unlocked the rear door and unstrapped the baby from its seat and raced to safety. I didn't even have time to check if the baby was okay. I put the baby on the grass and went back to try and help the couple. It was almost impossible to see anything. Smoke was billowing from the hood, the heat was unbearable, and just as I reached your father's open window the entire front of the car went up in flames."

Eli's mother started crying softly; his father put an arm around her shoulder.

*"Just as I got near the car, flames shot out from under the hood."*

Eli kept picturing the scene of the accident. A dark mountain road. A crash. The smell of gasoline. A baby saved from the fire...

He thought of the blessing of the kabbalist and suddenly it hit him: He was that baby!

They were talking about his parents. His real parents had been inside that burning car!

Chapter 2

# The Rabbi's Request

The judges of the religious court of Tzfat had awarded Harry and Eileen Bloome custody of the infant that had survived the accident. The Bloomes had agreed to the court's request that they tell Eli about his identity on his Bar Mitzvah.

That was part of the reason Eli's Bar Mitzvah celebration was to take place in Israel. The Bloomes wanted to be with Eli when he paid his respects at the grave of his natural parents. They wanted to be there for him.

But now, their well thought-out plan had fallen apart. Rabbi Mordechai, Eli's grandfather, had sent this secretive letter a month before the scheduled trip to Israel. When Mr. Bloome had received the letter, he knew without opening it, who it was from. At the time of the adoption, Eli's grandfather had accepted the court's opinion that a man of his advancing years could not care for a baby. He had only asked Mr. and Mrs. Bloome to raise his grandson according to Jewish law and bring him to

Israel when he came of age.

He could have waited one more month, Mr. Bloome thought to himself. It wouldn't have been too much to ask. Then, almost at the same instant, he knew the answer. Eli had already passed his Hebrew birthday. Technically, he was 13. He had been called up to the Torah in the synagogue only last week, even though he had chosen to read from the Torah when in Israel.

The old rabbi probably thought we were going back on our word, Mr. Bloome reasoned. That's why he sent the letter.

"Eli," Mr. Bloome said out loud, "your grandfather was there when we adopted you. You are his last living relative. We agreed to his condition of bringing you to Israel for your Bar Mitzvah. We also feel it's important to pay your respects at the grave of your natural parents."

"The court in Tzfat respected your grandfather very much," his mother said. "They warned us to honor all his requests."

"But how did he know to send the letter now?"

"You've turned 13," said his mother. "He's probably been counting the days."

"And what about my — my — ?"

"Your natural parents?" his father offered. "They would have been our age now, had they lived. Your father was a Bible scholar at Bar Ilan University and your mother was a medical student. They were on their way home after a short vacation. More than that I don't know. I wish we had more information for you."

Eli sat in a daze.

"You can go to Israel before the Bar Mitzvah," his mother suggested, "and spend a few weeks with your grandfather if you like."

"I don't know," said Eli, slowly rising from the table. "I need some time. It's so incredible."

Eli went to his room and sat on his bed. He looked at his Yankees team picture, his historical map of the ancient world, his posters of the Sinai Desert and the Canadian Rockies.

The room no longer seemed like his own. He felt like a stranger suddenly dropped into someone else's life. Abruptly, he went outside and climbed into his tree fort high in the chestnut tree in the backyard. He found his favorite branch and dangled his legs into space. He stared through the leaves into the night sky. The stars seemed shrouded in mist. They blurred and then came back into focus. He squinted and then realized he was seeing the heavens through his tears.

## Chapter 3

# Journey to the Holy Land

For a few days Eli turned the strange story over in his mind. He wished he could go back in time — just a week — to when his life seemed safe and simple. But there was no turning back. His grandfather across the ocean was waiting to meet him.

His Saba. He mulled the word over in his mind. The Hebrew word began to sound like a name. He wondered who this old man was behind the letter.

Eli decided to go to Israel before his parents. It would only be for a week or two and he wouldn't be alone. Mr. Bloome had called Rabbi Mordechai to make arrangements. The old man said he would send his friend, a taxi driver named Moshe, to meet Eli at Ben Gurion Airport.

At J.F.K., Eli's parents kissed him goodbye and told him to call every day. They would soon join him in Tzfat and then they would travel to Jerusalem for his Bar Mitzvah at the Western Wall.

Eli had never flown before. After the excitement of

take-off, he settled down and took out a Bible from his bag. He turned the well-worn pages to his favorite story, the tale of King Saul and the Witch of Endor. This episode had always fascinated him. How could the King of Israel visit a witch? Wasn't fortune-telling forbidden? Hadn't Saul himself outlawed such practices? But King Saul was desperate to know the outcome of his impending battle with the Philistines. Would he meet his death in this war? He had to know.

If I were going to die, Eli thought, I wouldn't want to know about it. Let it come when it comes. Like it did ... with my parents. His mind wandered to his grandfather's letter which he had put in the front flap of his backpack. He had read the letter over and over. One sentence jumped out at him each time: *You must be prepared to receive your inheritance.*

Prepare? How? Eli wondered. He tried to imagine his grandfather, his natural parents and the life they had lived in Israel. As the jet soared over the Atlantic he felt he was soaring back in time. Back to the moment when a baby cried out from the smoke and flames.

## Chapter 4

# Moshe the Taxi Driver

Ben Gurion Airport hummed with the excitement of a huge family reunion. Everywhere in the terminal people were hugging, kissing, laughing and crying.

He asked the man at the taxi stand if he had seen a driver named Moshe from Tzfat.

"Tzfat? Three hundred shekels."

"No, you don't understand," said Eli. "My grandfather sent a driver named Moshe from Tzfat."

The attendant's face puckered as if he had eaten a sour pickle. "Moshe? Over there." He pointed to a long row of taxis by a curb.

Eli frowned and lugged his suitcase over to where the taxis were waiting. "Moshe from Tzfat?" he asked them, "Moshe from Tzfat?"

Five drivers answered to the name Moshe. All were anxious to go to Tzfat, but none of them were from Tzfat.

His Moshe was probably late, but how long would he

have to wait? Eli watched a young boy walking with his parents. For a moment, he started to feel homesick. But he pushed the feeling away. His journey was just beginning. He had to be strong.

An hour later, an old olive-green Mercedes came chugging down the road. It was covered with dust and gray clay and looked as if it had not only come out of the mountains, but had brought some of the mountains with it. The luggage rack on the roof was rusted and the hubcaps were missing. The traditional Mercedes hood ornament had been replaced by a small chrome soccerball. Eli went over to the driver's window.

"Moshe from Tzfat?"

"Eli from New York? Shalom Aleichem!" Eli shook the driver's outstretched hand. The man's warmth rekindled Eli's excitement for the journey.

"Your Saba is waiting for you," said Moshe. "Let's go."

The old cab coughed black smoke as it pulled away from the curb. Moshe pushed a tape into the cassette player; an oriental tune blared. To Eli it sounded like music that might flow through an Arab shuk or marketplace. Flowering date palms rushed by. Before long, a sea breeze blew in through the open windows.

One hand on the steering wheel, Moshe turned around to ask, "You know who Rabbi Mordechai is don't you?" Before Eli could answer, Moshe added, "Your grandfather is a *tzaddik*, a great man. A great man!" he repeated, for emphasis. "You don't know how lucky you are."

Eli opened his mouth to say something — of course he knew his grandfather was a great man — but decided against it. An oncoming truck, even more dilapidated than Moshe's relic, honked as their taxi crossed into the oncoming lane. Moshe looked forward and expertly straightened out the car again. However, now he looked at Eli through the rearview mirror.

"Of course you don't know. But you should. Your grandfather is one of the 36 hidden righteous ones."

Thirty-six hidden righteous ones? Is that something I'm supposed to know about? thought Eli.

"In every generation," Moshe went on, "there are 36 righteous men, 36 *tzadikkim*. All the generation stands on their shoulders."

For a moment Eli pictured a pyramid of 36 gray-bearded old men in flowing robes balanced on each other's shoulders. At the top of the pyramid stood one man — his grandfather — with the weight of the world resting solidly upon him. He resisted laughing at the image he had conjured up, not because it would insult Moshe, but because somehow he sensed it rang true.

"Israel is always in danger," Moshe said ominously. "If it weren't for those 36, who knows what would happen!"

He lowered his voice. "Maybe your grandfather called you to Israel to help him. Have you thought of that?"

Eli shook his head. He honestly didn't think the head of the 36 righteous ones would need his help for anything.

"Everyone in Tzfat has a different story about why

*At the top of the pyramid stood one man — his grandfather — with the weight of the world resting solidly upon him.*

your grandfather has settled there, but I know the real reason. Do you want to know the truth about your Saba?"

This time Eli nodded his head, yes.

"Rabbi Mordechai is here, in Tzfat, to remove the curse of Jaktabar, the Sorcerer," Moshe announced, like a man revealing the Messiah to the world.

Eli didn't move in his seat. He remembered the letter. The words that perhaps alluded to a curse. *You must know there is an evil within and an evil without* his grandfather had written. He hadn't taken it all too seriously. But now, for the first time, Eli was scared.

Eli decided he had heard enough. He closed his eyes, pretending to sleep. Moshe talked a bit more, but when he saw his audience asleep, he went back to watching the road.

They traveled Highway 1 north along the coast towards Haifa. Eli slowly opened his eyes, careful not to make a sound. He peered out the window. Everywhere there were signs of a new country and an old country growing side-by-side. Buildings rose out of sand dunes beside the stones of ancient ruins. Highways criss-crossed what were once old caravan routes. Billboards advertised Cable TV while on the street below, an old man sold goat's milk from a jug strapped to a donkey.

Eli felt he was somehow part of this country. He was in fact, an Israeli citizen, a sabra. His parents had always insisted he learn to read and speak Hebrew fluently. Now he knew why.

Eli smiled as he remembered what Rabbi Stein, his

Hebrew language tutor had said:

"A sabra is a desert fruit. It has a tough leathery skin, full of little thorns, but the fruit inside is sweet and juicy. It has saved many a wanderer lost in the desert. Perhaps that is why native born Israelis are called sabras. They too have tough exteriors, but inside are sweet and caring. And, whenever they are lost in this world they reach inside themselves and drink of their heritage."

Is that what I am, Eli thought, a sabra? I sure don't feel like one. And yet, in a strange, unexplainable way, I feel like this is home.

Moshe broke into Eli's thoughts with a sudden warning. "We must pass the village of Jaktabar on our way to Tzfat."

"What kind of village is that?" Eli asked.

"You will see and then you will know," was the cabby's cryptic answer.

After another hour they turned inland off the highway and headed towards the hills dividing the coast from the rest of the country.

"There are three things a man must suffer to acquire," the cabby quoted: "Torah. The World to Come. And the land of Israel."

"Torah is the Jewish Bible, what non-Jews call the Old Testament."

"I know what the Torah is," Eli told him, annoyed at being talked down to.

Without warning, Moshe drew a pistol from beneath his seat.

"There are people here who don't want us to acquire

the land of Israel, even though we already have. They want to kill us," he said, holding the pistol up high so Eli could see it. "We must be prepared to defend ourselves."

This fellow is definitely weird, and dangerous, Eli thought.

A few moments later they were on the outskirts of a village. The road sign was in Hebrew and Arabic. Eli could just make out the Hebrew letters: "Jaktabar."

A large crowd was gathered in the middle of the single road that passed through the village. Old women balanced baskets of vegetables and herbs on their heads. Young boys hawked drinks, cakes and candies. A group of men sat in a circle. Then Eli saw a man running with a snake in his hand. The snake was huge and it's tail dragged in the dust. Children were chasing after the man, beating the snake with white sticks. Then Eli looked closer and saw that the sticks were bones.

Nearby, some foreign journalists were filming the whole event. They seemed very interested in the snake and the bones. One of them, speaking Arabic, seemed to be coaxing one of the children to hit the snake again, so the cameraman could take more film.

Further away, Eli caught a glimpse of a man with a black and silver caftan wearing a white turban on his head. People were lined up before him. An old man was kneeling at his feet. Men with automatic rifles were standing beside the man in the caftan.

"Who's that, up there?" asked Eli.

"Jaktabar, himself. He comes out in the evening sometimes to 'bless' his people. I spit on him!" To em-

*Then Eli saw a man running with a snake in his hand. The snake was huge and it's tail dragged in the dust. Children were chasing after the man, beating the snake with white sticks.*

phasize his words, Moshe spat out the window.

As though by some prearranged plan, several Arab youths broke from the crowd that had gathered around Jaktabar and rushed the taxi. Moshe raised the gun and stepped on the gas. The old Mercedes lurched ahead of the gang. They shouted curses and unleashed a shower of stones. Eli ducked beneath the window as a stone struck the car door and Moshe fired a shot in the air.

The taxi scrambled quickly down the road past the village.

Moshe was silent again. Bright beads of sweat showed on his forehead. His eyes were set on the road ahead.

"Never be afraid of anything but God," he announced. "When I tell you this, I am telling myself also." He put the gun back under his seat.

Eli slowly straightened up. He looked down and saw that his hands were gripping the door handle. Fortunately, the door lock was pushed down or he would have certainly fallen out of the taxi.

"That man is a sorcerer," said Moshe. "He blames the Jews for all the problems of his village and fills the villagers with hate. It is not a new story."

"Is he really a sorcerer?" Eli wondered out loud. He was still trembling and it seemed like his heart would never slow down.

"I have heard stories that he speaks with the dead."

"Why does he speak with the dead?"

"To know the future, of course," answered Moshe, slightly annoyed with Eli's naive question.

A chill ran down Eli's back. He wondered what his

grandfather could possibly expect him to do against such an enemy. How could he help fight a sorcerer? His visit no longer seemed a simple matter of paying respects and receiving an inheritance. Each step he took seemed to drag him deeper into a dark sinister affair for which he was unprepared and afraid.

He doubted his parents would have let him come, had they known about Jaktabar. In truth, he wasn't so sure he would have come himself...

Chapter 5

# Enemies in a Dream

From the city of Tzfat, high on a mountain in northern Israel, you can see the green hills of the Galilee rolling like waves to the Mediterranean. Tzfat is a city of ancient synagogues, mystics, and holy rabbis. On the side of the mountain that leads up to the city is a 1,000-year-old cemetery where, it is rumored, the 36 righteous of every generation come to be buried.

Moshe and Eli entered the city along the main road, past restaurants and shops and quaint old buildings. Then they left the modern section of the town and crossed into the Old City. Here the streets were paved with cobblestones and most of the homes were centuries old. There were art galleries, pottery shops, weaving studios, and jewelry makers. Many of the people he saw in the streets looked very religious. They were dressed in dark suits or long robes. Women covered their hair and the men had long beards. The children's side-locks called *payot* bounced like springs as they ran down the street. At home Eli had heard of these Hasidic Jews, and even saw them at the shopping mall once in a while. But he had never spoken to them.

It suddenly occurred to Eli that Judaism in America was, at best, a part of a Jew's everyday life. But in the Old City of Tzfat, Judaism was life itself.

Moshe dropped Eli off on a worn path at the edge of the cemetery. He pointed to an old stone house which was nearly in ruins, jutting out of the hillside.

"There," he said. "If Rabbi Mordechai is not home, wait for him. He will come."

Eli thanked the driver and took his bags out of the car. After the taxi pulled away, the only sound he could hear was a faint breeze high in the pine trees. Strange, he thought, I feel like I know this place.

The old stone house had a domed roof. Yellow flowers sprang from cracks in the mortar. The windows were dark and set deep in the wall.

The house itself was built into the hill at the edge of the cemetery. There were no neighbors on either side, only more ruins. The yard was littered with stones like an ancient quarry.

Eli went to the door and knocked, but there was no answer. He tried again. Still no one came. He set down his bags and peered in a window, but all he could see was his reflection in the glass.

Suddenly a cat snarled and Eli jumped up in fright, knocking his head against the stone archway of the window. Sparks of light swirled before him and then...darkness.

Out of the darkness a band of wild men appeared. They ran through the Old City of Tzfat as the city burst into flames. Cold, black eyes glittered with rage, hatchets and knives dripped with blood, and torches were hurled onto rooftops. The men wore the traditional Arab kafiyas, part of the material pulled over their faces as they shouted their anger into the wind. Eli knew they were coming for him, but he could not move. There was nowhere to hide. In desperation, he screamed...

And the vision vanished. In its place stood an old man with a white beard with dark leathery skin, blazing blue eyes, and the warmest smile Eli had ever seen, or felt. He was gently holding Eli up.

"Shalom," said the old man in a soft, warm voice. "Do not fear. Our enemies cannot hurt us now."

Eli stared at him. "Our enemies?" But Eli was sure they were after him and him alone. And how did this old man know what he was dreaming about?

"It's easier to enter a house through the door," the old man went on, leading Eli to the front door.

"I am your Saba," Rabbi Mordechai introduced himself as they stood in the little vestibule leading into the two rooms that made up the entire house. "And you are my grandson, Eli."

Eli nodded and tried to extend his hand. But he was still groggy and almost tripped over himself. With the speed and agility of someone half his age, Eli's grandfather ran to his side and led him to a couch. Eli flopped down and touched his head. A sizeable bump met his fingers.

Rabbi Mordechai went to the back of the room where a refrigerator stood beside a counter. He took out several plates of food and set them on the table. Eli watched him curiously.

This is one of the 36 righteous men? Eli wondered. He looks like a shoemaker.

They ate in silence. Rabbi Mordechai made the appropriate blessings over each type of food he ate. At the end of the meal he gazed at Eli but seemed to be looking far beyond.

"You came a long way to visit someone you don't even know," Rabbi Mordechai said. "You have great courage."

Eli looked down in embarrassment.

His Saba sighed. "When there is too much to say, it is best to say nothing."

Rabbi Mordechai took a prayerbook from a little shelf of old volumes. The pages were brittle and yellowed.

After praying he kissed the book and selected another volume. As he read, he chanted the verses in a soft voice. Eli watched the way his grandfather turned the pages, lifting each one slowly and laying it to rest, as though uncovering a long hidden treasure.

"What should I call you?" Eli asked when the old man paused for moment.

"Call me Saba," he said. "I have had that name for 13 years now, but no one to speak it. A person can only become his name when he hears it often. Then he can wear it like comfortable clothes."

Eli didn't quite understand what his grandfather was

getting at, but right now, he was more interested in his own history than words of wisdom.

"Can you tell me about my parents, Saba?" he asked.

The old man lowered his head as if it had suddenly grown heavy.

"They were good Jews. They accomplished what they were meant to."

"And what was that?"

"You are their accomplishment," Saba answered matter-of-factly.

Eli shifted in his seat, uncomfortable with this answer. "But why did they have to die like that?"

Saba's eyes narrowed. "Why do you have to know?"

Eli blinked away tears. "They were my parents. Don't I have a right to know?"

A stern expression passed across Saba's face.

"Don't I?" Eli pressed.

"Now is not the time."

"You mean you know? And you won't tell me?"

"All knowledge must have a purpose," said Saba. "When you discover the true purpose, you will discover the knowledge." He breathed deeply several times, then smiled. "We have spoken enough. We will go now to the holy spring of the Ari HaKadosh. To cleanse ourselves of this day and prepare for the next one. Then I will take you to where your parents are buried."

Saba took Eli to the icy underground spring which was the *mikveh*, the pure waters in which the famous kabbalist, Rabbi Issac Luria, bathed and purified himself.

"Tradition has it," Rabbi Mordechai explained as they

entered a room carved out of the mountain, "that after the great Ari HaKadosh, whose real name was Isaac Luria, came to Tzfat, he entered a small cave at the base of the mountain. He wanted to ritually cleanse himself. To do this he searched for a pool of natural water. When he couldn't find it, the Ari, like Moses in the Bible, hit a stone and water poured out. This water still flows today and is the source of the spring water in the ritual bath."

Rabbi Mordechai took off his robe and stepped quickly into the cold water, dunking his entire body seven times. Then he emerged and dressed. Seeing Eli hesitate, Saba motioned for him to go in, but Eli was too embarrassed, and the water looked like it was ready to turn into ice.

"Next time, maybe," Eli mumbled, turning toward the entrance.

Saba looked at him and said, "Next time, you will go in."

When they left the *mikveh* a man approached them and asked Saba for a blessing. Saba placed his right hand on the man's head, closed his eyes, and whispered a prayer. The man pressed some money in Rabbi Mordechai's palm, kissed his hand and thanked him.

"Why did he do that?" Eli asked.

"Whoever you bless will be blessed," Saba quoted.

"No," Eli corrected, "I mean why did he give you money? Do blessings cost money?"

"Blessings are from God," Saba told him. "But the righteous know that they do not deserve the blessings of God. So, when they receive a blessing they also do a *mitzvah* — a commandment from the Torah — of giving *tzedaka*, a form of charity."

"I see," Eli said, not sounding convinced.

"You don't see yet," Saba said. "But you will, my beloved, you will."

They walked silently along the boundary of the cemetery. Over the centuries, Tzfat had been struck with several major earthquakes. Hundreds had died and it was rumored that beneath each house, two or even three layers of houses lay buried. The cemetery had also been damaged, headstones lay scattered about the hillside.

At the graves of several famous rabbis, Saba stopped and whispered prayers. Then he shared with Eli stories about the great men buried there.

At the bottom of the cemetery, they came to a section where the plots were neatly ordered and the headstones looked newer. Saba led Eli to a plot with a double headstone. The inscription was in Hebrew, and Eli slowly read the names out loud.

"Rivkah bat Esther. Aharon ben Shimon." He knew these were his parents. Eli tried to imagine what his parents had looked like, but his mind was blank. Staring at the headstones he let his mind wander, picturing how his life might have changed had the tragic accident that took his parents' lives not occurred. He began feeling sorry for himself. Then, looking up he noticed Saba weeping. Eli felt ashamed. How could he have forgotten that these were Saba's own daughter and son-in-law?

The old rabbi bent his head and whispered in his ear, *"Nachamu, B'ni, nachamu,* Be comforted, my son, be comforted."

## Chapter 6
# The Witch and the Prophet

That night Eli tried to call his parents.

"We're sorry we're not home to receive your call—" he heard his own voice say. He remembered he had taped the message only a few months ago. It felt strange leaving a message on the machine. He had the urge to echo his own words and say, "I'm sorry you're not home to receive my call," but resisted.

After he left a short message saying he was all right, Eli suddenly felt that a wide chasm had opened between himself and his parents. He was not sure where he belonged. He had only known Rabbi Mordechai, his Saba, for half a day and yet he felt a strange bond growing between them.

Eli wasn't sleepy so he opened his Bible to the section of King Saul and the Witch of Endor.

Rabbi Mordechai walked over to him. "What are you learning?"

"About King Saul and the Witch of Endor."

"What do you understand?"

Eli searched for the right words. "King Saul had passed a law that made it illegal to use magic. But when he had to go to battle, he was afraid he would die and wanted to ask the witch to show him the future."

"Very good," said Saba. "Our sages teach that the witch did not really bring up the soul of Samuel the Prophet. It was God himself who made the dead prophet appear. He gave King Saul one last prophecy so he'd have a chance to prove himself. Would he go into battle together with his sons, knowing they would all meet their deaths, or would he run away and bring shame upon the nation of Israel?"

Eli trembled, knowing that Saba was asking him the same question. Would he run away? Or stay and possibly...

Rabbi Mordechai began to study his own books as Eli tried to read some more. However, before he knew it, he fell asleep.

Again Eli dreamed of the band of wild men. Again they were rampaging through the burning city. They rushed past him waving torches, axes and knives, as he ducked behind a wall. They were heading for a synagogue. Eli heard terrible screams, windows smashing and furniture crashing. Then, silence. The band emerged from the synagogue like tigers sated from a kill, and roamed down the street. Eli was afraid of what he would find inside the synagogue. But a voice told him, "Go and see what they have done to your family." He turned into the entranceway and cried out in terror. Five old sages lay on the floor in a pool of blood. They were still wearing their prayer shawls and *tefillin*. One of them stirred, gasping for breath. Eli knelt beside him and the old man took Eli's hand.

"Hear, O Israel, the Lord our God, the Lord is One," the sage intoned.

After this he glared into Eli's eyes and said the Hebrew words, *"Aseh mishpat."* With that the image evaporated.

Eli awoke to find Saba holding his hand.

*"Aseh Mishpat* means, do justice," he said.

Eli withdrew in fear. How did his grandfather know what the man in his dream had said?

"Don't be afraid," said Saba.

"But how did you know?"

"You have a television, don't you?"

"Yeah," Eli said.

"You know the machine that sends pictures to the television?"

Eli nodded.

"This," Saba pointed to his head, "is the machine that sends pictures in a dream."

Eli started, "You mean *you* put that dream in my head?"

Saba looked as though he had been caught at some mischief.

"You are upset?" he asked.

"No. Well, I don't understand. It was a terrible dream."

"The old man who spoke to you was my grandfather. You are his great-great grandson. And you have an important job to do."

"Me?" Eli whispered.

Saba went to the kitchen and brought back two cups of hot tea. Saba sipped his tea slowly and then went on.

"One hundred and fifty years ago, the Jews of Tzfat were simple people. The city was on the trade route between Acco and Damascus, and for thousands of years, caravans would travel from the port of Acco across the land of Israel to places which had no access to the sea. Wadi Amud, which you saw yesterday, used to be a trade route. The caravans were often robbed by nomads who roamed the country in search of food and money.

"At that time, the Jews were under the rule of the Turks. They were many years of peace, but every once in a while, the Arabs living nearby would become restless. The men you saw in your dream came to Tzfat and destroyed the city. They murdered hundreds — old men, women and children. My father, Rabbi Ya'acov ben Orah, was a great tzaddik, a righteous sage who knew all the teachings of the Torah by heart. He died because he was a Jew. To this day, his soul is not at rest."

"What can I do?" asked Eli.

Saba took hold of his beard and said, "For every one of these hairs I have prayed a hundred prayers for you to come home. You were taken from me because I was old and alone, and I could not have cared for you properly. But you are not a child any longer. You are my soul and my flesh, just as we are the soul and the flesh of Rabbi Ya'acov. He comes to me, you know, and he asks, 'When, Rabbi Mordechai, when will there be justice?' I tell him soon, Rabbi Ya'acov, soon. When God brings our grandson back to the holy land."

Rabbi Mordechai wept. Then he dried his tears with a handkerchief. "Now that you are here," he said, "the time has come."

"But how can we do justice for Rabbi Ya'acov?" asked Eli. "That was so long ago."

Saba stared out the window cut into the thick stone walls as if it were the window of a prison.

"Just as we are the descendants of Rabbi Ya'acov, so are there sons from the sorcerer, Jaktabar. He is the murderer who led his band through our city and murdered Rabbi Ya'acov. Mufti Jaktabar was a sorcerer, a witch. To the Arabs in this area his word was law, and he put many hundreds to death on a whim. He and his band would ride through the wadis and attack caravans. He would curse people with his evil powers and most of the Jews and Turks feared him. But Rabbi Ya'acov had the courage to stand up to him, and that's why he was murdered. This is the way of the Other Side."

"The Other Side?"

"The forces of evil. Those who seek to destroy goodness and holiness."

"But, I thought—I thought—"

"You thought what? My son, you are young, you have not begun to look into the Torah and see the secrets there. Today people are taken in by the illusions of this world. Who understands the world of souls and the world of angels? Eli, you are here to help fulfill the prophecy of Rabbi Ya'acov. He predicted someone would come four generations after him to repair what was damaged.

These are the words of the Torah: God will withhold punishment up to the fourth generation. If, by then, the great-great grandchildren of a man have continued in the evil ways of their forefathers, God will bring down mighty punishment.

"You saw the man in charge of that village? He is the fourth generation of Jaktabar. He is the descendant of the one who murdered your great-great grandfather. He continues in the ways of his fathers, turning his people against the Jews and using the powers of the Other Side."

"Does Jaktabar know about the prophecy of the fourth generation?"

Saba sighed.

"And that I'm the one —?"

Saba closed his eyes, nodding.

Eli felt a cold wind blow deep into his heart. He wished he had kept his face hidden from the Arab youths they had confronted.

"But do not be afraid, Eli. You will be blessed. And we will work together for Rabbi Ya'acov. For all our people.

"Before Rabbi Ya'acov left this world, he already knew what would become of him, and of us. So he left a will with instructions about the treasure he had buried."

The inheritance, Eli thought. Now he knew why Saba had written in his letter, *To see if you are prepared.*

"But do not think only of the treasure," Saba warned. "Our work is to put an end to the son of Jaktabar."

Chapter 7

# The Weeping Sisters

Early the next morning there was a loud knock at the door. Rabbi Mordechai greeted three young women of dark complexion, wearing long dresses with their hair pulled back tightly. One spoke swiftly, in Hebrew, to Saba. Eli understood that the sisters were afraid of something and were asking for help.

Saba gave them some instructions and they hurried away.

Rabbi Mordechai returned to his chair. "You see?" he said. "Our work has already begun."

"What did they want?"

"They want to get married," said Saba.

Eli had a sinking feeling. "Aren't I a little young —?"

"They think someone put the Evil Eye on them," Saba continued, ignoring Eli's half-asked question. "They think that's why they can't find husbands."

"The Evil Eye?" Eli asked, relieved that his fears of early marriage were unfounded.

Rabbi Mordechai did not answer.

Suddenly Eli knew. "It has something to do with Jaktabar?"

Rabbi Mordechai rubbed his eyes.

"The sisters have prayed and prayed. Each time they thought they found the right man, something has happened to destroy their plans. They asked themselves. We all wonder. Why shouldn't they be married already? Unless it's as you say, Jaktabar has cursed them."

"To never get married?"

"The sisters live in a place famous for troubles. The House of Mourning it is called. There is a well inside the house. I told them to check if anything strange has occurred at the well."

"And if they find something?"

"Then we will have to look inside."

Soon the sisters returned. Rabbi Mordechai spoke to them, went to wash his hands, then sat at his writing table. He took an old velvet bag from the drawer and produced a quill, a glass jar of ink and a small square of parchment. After saying a prayer, Saba wrote Hebrew letters on the parchment and waited for the ink to dry. Then he rolled it up and slipped it into a silver vial. Motioning for Eli to come closer he lay the vial in his hand.

"It is as we suspected. Put this parchment in the sisters' well." Saba gave him a canvas bag. "Gather whatever comes to the surface of the water and put it in this bag. Then bring it back to me, quickly."

Eli put the vial in his pocket and slung the bag over his

shoulder. Saba walked him to the door.

"Eli," he said, "you are my legs, my arms and my eyes. Do not be afraid. God is with you."

Eli left with the sisters. They walked up the road along the mountain and turned down a lane which led into the heart of the Old City. It was not long before they came to a narrow staircase leading to a courtyard overgrown with aloes and grapevines.

Inside the cool dark house, Eli saw a shelf filled with candles and family pictures. There *was* something creepy about the House of Mourning. Like its name, it seemed filled with lost hopes, disappointments and loneliness.

The eldest sister took him down to the cellar. It was damp and dark, except for a crack of light from a boarded-up window. Brushing away the cobwebs which hung from the low ceiling, she bent down and pulled up a trap door.

"Here," she said in English. "The water comes from here."

Eli took out the flashlight he had brought with him from the States and pointed the beam inside the well. He did not see any water.

"This *is* serious," Eli said, visibly disturbed. "All your water is gone!"

The three sisters giggled in unison. "You have to go down," the eldest said, pointing towards a waterpipe that went into the shaft. "The water is below."

Eli took a deep breath. "There's no ladder," he said.

One of the other sisters crossed the cellar and brought back a thick rope. She tied it to a bar on the window and handed the other end to Eli. Eli let it fall into the well. He checked the knot on the window bars then placed the flashlight in his mouth and lowered himself slowly down into the wet, slimy darkness.

The only light was the narrow flashlight beam pointing out of his mouth. If he dropped the flashlight into the well, he would be in total darkness. Eli moved down slowly, then feeling a sneeze coming on, he bit hard on the flashlight and wiggled his nose. The feeling went away.

When his feet hit bottom, he took the light and swept the beam in a circle. He was standing in the center of an underground room. He followed the waterpipe with the flashlight to a large hole with water. Taking the vial from his pocket, he pulled off the top, slipped out the parchment and dropped it in. Then he waited.

Eli looked around. The room had a domed ceiling and stone walls. On one side was an archway loosely blocked with stones. Eli heard a bubbling sound. It sounded like a sea monster coming up to the surface of a lake. Water started shooting up like a fountain. It was churning up the well's contents below.

Eli aimed his flashlight and saw something slowly rising in the thick foam. He kept himself from panicking by sheer willpower. With a mighty effort he knelt down to get a closer look. White sticks danced in the middle of the water. He thought his eyes were playing tricks on him. But then the gurgling fountain began to die down and the sticks came to rest on a bed of greenish slime.

The bleached sticks were not sticks at all.

They were human bones.

*Eli aimed his flashlight and saw something slowly rising in the thick foam.*

## Chapter 8

# Clues to the Curse

Gingerly, Eli reached into the slime and pulled out a long white bone. His hand trembled. He forced himself to continue collecting the bones and shoving them into the canvas bag. There were five in all. When the last was in the bag, the water took on an eery calm. Eli stared into the water, wishing he were away from the House of Mourning, back in Saba's living room.

Slinging the canvas bag over his shoulder, Eli grasped the rope and got ready to climb. But then, his eyes caught a glimmer of light shining from behind the archway. Saba's words came back to him: "You are my legs, my arms, and my eyes." He didn't want to, but he felt Saba would want him to investigate.

"Okay down there?" came the muffled voice of the woman above.

"Fine, just a few more minutes."

Eli went to the archway and easily pushed out a few stones. Soon there was an opening he could climb

through. Inside he saw what must once have been someone's room. Two beams, fallen from the ceiling, had
crushed a table and some chairs. There was an old
wooden barrel against a wall, a small desk, a stove built
of stones, a fallen bookshelf and the frame of a single
bed. He looked inside the barrel. Ashes, dust, cobwebs
and more stones. He went to the desk and pulled open a
drawer. Inside was an envelope stuffed with papers. The
papers had undecipherable Hebrew writing on them,
with strange signs and diagrams drawn on their margins.
Eli gently put the envelope in his back pocket then tied
the noose of the canvas bag to his belt and slung it over
his shoulder. He climbed back through the archway and
seized the rope.

"Coming up," he called.

Climbing hand over hand, Eli reached the top of the
shaft, his arms and legs, sore from the exertion, scraped
and bruised from the stones of the shaft. All three sisters
were waiting for him. One held a tray with cakes and a
teapot, another had a towel and sponge. The eldest sister
was rolling the rope. It was an odd scene, the sisters
standing there as if it were teatime. He shifted the bag
further back on his shoulder.

"You found something?" asked the eldest sister, staring at the bulging bag.

"You'll have to ask Saba," Eli answered, shifting the
bag again, as though hiding it behind him.

"Can't you tell us what you found?" she pleaded.

He wasn't going to be the one to tell them they'd
been drinking water from a well filled with bones. He

glanced at the steaming kettle but decided now was not the time to stop for tea. The young women followed him up the staircase to the kitchen.

"Please tell us what you are taking back to your Saba," the middle sister pleaded. "We have been waiting so long for an answer to our prayers."

"I'm sorry," said Eli, as he started for the door.

Seeing how upset the sisters were, Eli hit upon an idea.

"But I can tell you one thing," he volunteered.

"What is it?" the oldest sister echoed. "You can trust us," she said, looking at her siblings who both nodded their agreement.

"Well," Eli whispered, "I think Rabbi Mordechai is about to perform a miracle for you. Very soon you should all meet your husbands and have three wonderful weddings."

"Amen!" the sisters chimed together like three happy bells.

Eli turned and started for the door.

"Are you sure you won't have a drink, some water?" asked the youngest sister.

"No thank you," Eli said with a bow. He was trotting down the street before they could pressure him further.

Outside, in the warm sunlight, he felt like Indiana Jones or some great explorer who had just located a secret treasure. The aches and pains, scrapes and bruises, now felt like medals of valor earned in battle. He would have loved to tell his parents about his adventure, but they would probably laugh at his tale of bones and curses and sorcerers. Or worse, they might tell him to take the next flight home.

Eli noticed a group of Arab workers at a construction site a few doors down from the House of Mourning. They wore kafiyas around their heads and scowled at him. They looked surprisingly like the youths who had charged the taxi in Jaktabar.

As he hurried in the direction of Saba's house, a moss green taxi with a chrome soccer ball on the hood rambled towards him on HaAri Street.

Rabbi Mordechai's grandson, how are you?" called Moshe. "You want a ride?"

Eli climbed in the front seat, keeping a tight grip on the canvas bag.

"What's in the bag?" Moshe asked.

"Nothing," Eli answered, suddenly sorry he had decided to accept Moshe's offer for a ride.

"Nu? You hold it like it was the treasures of Sulleiman, the Turkish Caliph who once ruled —." Moshe stopped, realizing that Eli was not rising to the bait.

Eli stared ahead through the windshield.

"Of course it is none of my business," Moshe admitted. "But you should know, your grandfather trusts me more than anyone in this town. I am the one who takes him to Meron to pray at the grave of Rabbi Shimon bar Yochai! I am the one who takes him to the cave of Rava and Abbaye. We have learned the secrets of the Kabbalah together. We are very close. I would give my life for your grandfather."

"I'm sure he appreciates that," said Eli diplomatically.

"So, you *see*," said Moshe, "if you tell me it will not be a problem. It might even be a mitzvah, a good thing to do," the wiry driver told him.

Eli bit his lower lip. He did not want to hurt Moshe's feelings. On the other hand, Moshe might drive him around forever unless he told him something.

They turned a corner. Saba was standing on the edge of the road.

"Saved," Eli mumbled to himself.

"Shalom aleichem, Rabbi Mordechai," Moshe called out as he stopped the car.

Rabbi Mordechai smiled.

"Moshe," he said, "You should not worry yourself with things that do not concern you."

The words, though spoken gently, turned Moshe's face white. He took Saba's hand and said, "I'm sorry Saba. I was only curious. I wanted to help."

"I know," Saba answered. "But there will be other times for you to help."

Eli heard Moshe call his grandfather "Saba" and suddenly realized that in Tzfat all the people were Saba's children, and they revered him like their own grandfather.

Eli said goodbye to Moshe and followed Saba into his house. Once inside, Saba carefully opened the bag and spread its contents on a cloth on the table.

Eli watched Saba examine each bone. He held them up to the light, turning them this way and that until he found what he was looking for.

"Here," he said, pointing to some scratch marks in a

length of bone. "This is the sign of Jaktabar."

"What does it say?"

"It's a curse on the water of the Jews."

"Why water?" Eli asked.

"Water is the source of life," Rabbi Mordechai explained. "A curse on water cuts off the blessings of life. That is why the sisters were not yet married, for the purpose of marriage is to bring new life into the world."

Saba gathered the bones into the bag and took out paper and pencil.

"Take this," he commanded, while writing, "and give it to the sisters together with the bones. They are to burn the bones and the note to ashes and cast them into the air around the house. Do not wait for them, but come home after you deliver the message."

Eli took the note and the canvas bag to the House of Mourning. The sisters took the bag and the note and carried it, like something holy, into their courtyard. He would have liked to watch them perform the ritual, but he remembered that Saba had told him to come home right away.

When he returned, Saba said to Eli, "Did you find anything else near the well?"

Eli had been so preoccupied with the bones that he had forgotten the old room and the papers in the envelope. He quickly reached into his back pocket and took out the envelope.

Saba examined the papers like an archeologist deciphering the ruins of an ancient civilization.

"Yes," nodded Saba. "Just as he said."

"Someone told you about these letters?" Eli asked.

"Rabbi Ya'acov."

"But he's —"

Rabbi Mordechai smiled.

"Remember, he visits us...if only in our dreams."

Eli was confused. "But how does he do it?"

"How does a song come over the radio? A wave of sound, yes? Well there are sound waves, and there are soul waves. Our ears gather sound waves, and our souls, if we merit it, gather waves of information from other souls."

"I wonder why my parents never came to me in a dream."

Saba folded the envelope into his coat. "You tell me."

"I don't know."

"Then think. This is what you are here for."

Eli closed his eyes and said the first thing that came to mind.

"Maybe it would have frightened me."

"Perhaps."

Eli suddenly wanted to cry. "Why else?" he pleaded feeling frustrated by Saba's way of teaching.

Saba laid a hand on his shoulder.

"Without training your ears to listen well, you cannot hear all there is to hear."

"I have to train myself to listen," Eli said. Then it became clear to him. "I have to train myself to listen...to my soul."

"Excellent," Saba said with a smile. "When you learn to listen you will hear the voice of all creation."

Chapter 9

# To Do and To Hear

After the evening prayer, Eli and Saba had dinner. Saba ate a few bites and put his plate in the sink. Eli continued eating. The more he grew to know Rabbi Mordechai, the more questions he wanted to ask him.

"Saba," he asked, "why do you eat so little? You're twice my size and I eat much more."

The old man smiled at him. "Why do you think?"

"I guess you're like a rocket—a little fuel goes a long way."

Saba laughed, then turned his attention to the envelope Eli had brought up from the ruins.

"The apartment you found today belonged to Rabbi Ya'acov," he said. "These are his papers and they tell where to find his personal treasures. It is our inheritance."

Eli stopped chewing and swallowed.

"The next step is to find the treasure before Jaktabar."

"How does he know about it?"

"It is part of his tradition. He believes that to regain his former power he must overcome Rabbi Ya'acov's family. Remember, before Israel's War of Independence, Arabs lived in Tzfat. They owned many of the houses, and the House of Morning was Jaktabar's own house, but he abandoned it during the war. It is one of God's ironies that while Jaktabar knew that Rabbi Ya'acov had lived somewhere in the area he didn't realize he himself was living directly above the great rabbi's house.

"We have fought for many years, Jaktabar and I." Rabbi Mordechai had a distant look in his eyes.

"How have you fought?" Eli asked quietly.

"Battles of the spirit, for lost souls, to cancel decrees, to earn merit for our people to survive. Sometimes I have won. Sometimes he has. But the bones have told me that now Jaktabar knows where the treasure is and he will do everything in his power to get it. This will be more than a battle for him, this will be his own personal *jihad*."

"A holy war," said Eli, remembering the word from the newspapers in America.

"A war that must be fought to the death."

Suddenly, Eli remembered something else he had seen near the sisters' house.

"Saba, outside the House of Mourning, I saw some Arabs working. Do you think they might be Jaktabar's men trying to enter Rabbi Ya'acov's room from another entrance? They looked a lot like the guys that stoned our cab."

"Where were they exactly?"

"On a house down the hill from the House of Mourning."

"Be very careful of them," Saba warned. "Especially do not look them in the eyes."

"Why the eyes?"

"Through the eyes enters fear. And he who protects his eyes, protects himself from the Evil Eye. You must guard yourself from fearing anything but God."

Outside, the wind rose in the pine trees, as if issuing a warning of its own.

"Saba, did you know all along that Rabbi Ya'acov's house was buried down there?"

Saba did not answer.

"I guess I was wondering why you didn't tell me," Eli continued. "It just seems like everything is a secret, and I'm the only one who doesn't really understand what's happening."

"*Na'ase v'nishma*," Eli's grandfather said. "We will do and we will hear. First we do, and then we understand. The Jewish people do what God commands and understand after."

Saba suddenly looked at Eli, as though with his gaze he could make his grandson understand something that mere words could not explain.

"To understand first and then to do, is the way of man, it is the way most people are raised. But to do first and then to understand is the way of the angels, it is the kabbalist's way, the way of belief. If you want to truly hear the messages of the soul, you must let your soul lead your mind. You must accept the words and commandments of God, as our forefathers did when they received the Torah and shouted, *Na'aseh v'nishma!*"

Eli didn't know why, but tears were flowing from his eyes. His Saba's words, still unclear to him, seemed to hold a truth his soul wanted desperately for him to accept.

Later in the day, Saba reminded Eli to call his parents again.

"How's it going, Eli?" his father's voice came over the line. "We're sorry we missed your call. Are you having fun?"

Eli told them about his plane trip and about the city of Tzfat.

"And how is your grandfather?" his mother asked, picking up the phone from another part of the house. "We were worried you might get bored. After all, he is an old man."

"I may be a lot of things here, but I'm not bored," he confided. "We're getting along fine."

"I'm happy to hear that," his mother said. "I mean, what can there be to do in a sleepy old town—?"

"We were a little concerned because of the terrorist attack," his father broke in.

"What attack?"

"You didn't hear? In some village in the North. Where was it honey, Jacktamar or something like that? A taxi filled with passengers was attacked while on vacation. There was even mention of a young boy in the taxi. We were very worried."

Eli swallowed hard.

"That's-uh-pretty bad, I hope they're okay. Must have scared those people." Eli realized that somehow the media had heard of the incident and exaggerated what had happened to him. They had an entire family being attacked, instead of one scared boy.

"So, do you miss us?" asked his Mother.

"Yeah, sure I do," said Eli. "I — uh, can't wait till you come."

"Neither can we. Has your grandfather said anything about your inheritance?"

"Well, not really, it's—"

"Not easy to speak of, I know. But he'll talk to you about it when he thinks your ready, I'm sure," his mother assured him. "He did say in the letter you would have to be prepared," she reminded him.

Eli grinned, thinking, if they only knew *how much* I still need to know and what I'm preparing for...

Chapter 10

# A Sabbath Tale

The next day was Friday. Saba spent the day studying and preparing for the Sabbath.

Eli wanted to know more about the documents he had found in the ruins of Rabbi Ya'acov's house, but it was clear that the approaching day of rest was the only thing on Saba's mind.

"After the Sabbath," he said to Eli, when the boy glanced at the envelope on the writing desk. "Today we prepare ourselves for the queen."

Eli washed the windows and swept the floors. He started to tidy up some books but Saba told him, "Those stay where they are. Each has its place. And time."

Eli learned what it meant to be organized. Everything in Saba's simple home had a place, and he knew when it was moved and not put back exactly right.

The furniture was very old, the rugs on the stone floor were worn, the few pictures on the walls were of great rabbis.

Eli wondered what Saba's wife had been like.

Later, while they walked through the cemetery on the way to the ritual bath, Eli said, "Saba, can you tell me about my grandmother?"

Saba stopped on the stone path and gazed straight ahead. Then he raised his eyes as though he were standing before an angel.

He remained frozen in that position for a long time. Tears came to his eyes. Finally, he walked on.

Eli remembered one of Saba's sayings:

*"When there is too much to say, it is best to say nothing."*

They passed grave after grave. So many dead people, thought Eli, where did they all go? It couldn't be they just vanished forever. There had to be some purpose, some greater goal. Maybe there was reincarnation, or afterlife for souls, like Newton's Law, which Eli had learned in Physics class: energy is never lost, it is merely changed into another form.

Saba stopped on the path beside an anthill.

"They are always building," he said. "To us it looks like a mound of sand. But to them it is the palace of their queen."

Saba looked at Eli, and Eli knew his grandfather was waiting for him to respond.

"So each of us is here to build a palace for the queen? The Sabbath Queen?"

Saba let out a shout of joy and praised God with five different Hebrew expressions. He danced a little step and then suddenly, as though he were catching himself at the edge of cliff, he froze. His face became clouded in shadows.

"Saba, what's wrong?" asked Eli.

"It is not fitting to act this way in a holy cemetery." He glanced up to heaven and uttered a prayer, then hurried down the path.

When they reached the *mikveh*, Eli agreed to enter the dark pool. The water was icy and dunking seven times, as Saba insisted, left him cold and shivering. But, strangely, when he stepped out of the mikveh he felt fresh and alive. The cold gave way to a warm feeling, a feeling of well-being he would keep with him throughout the Sabbath day.

Sabbath with Saba was an adventure Eli would never forget. Each commandment he performed was another step up a mountain — not a mountain of stone, but a mountain of spirit. There was a timeless sense about the entire day. They began by dressing in their finest clothes — Saba in a simple white robe, slippers and a white head-covering, Eli in his best blue suit. During evening prayers in the synagogue of the Ari, their voices rose with the birds that fluttered through the open windows of the synagogue, rested on its ancient rafters, and then continued their journey out into the heavens.

At home, Saba called Eli to his side, placed his hands on his head and blessed him. During *Kiddush*, the blessing over the wine, Saba stared into the cup as if it were a crystal ball that held the answers to all his questions. He raised two loaves of *challah* in front of him and blessed the Creator for bringing forth bread from the earth.

Then the meal began. Each course was introduced with a song. Saba had invited Moshe the taxi driver and his family to join them. When the main course was finished, Saba glanced around the table and blessed each person, ending with Eli.

"May the Almighty bless you," he said, "with the power to reveal to each man that God is within him. This is the hidden meaning of your name, Eli, Eliyahu." (Elijah the Prophet)

Then Saba leaned back in his chair.

"Now I will tell a story," he said.

There was once a king who lived in a magical kingdom called the Kingdom of Light. In this kingdom all were at peace. There was no war and no hatred. No jealousy and no envy. Impurity had no hold over this kingdom because a wondrous cloud protected it from all the evils of the world.

The king had two sons. One was good and the other was evil. The cloud, which was able to keep evil from entering the kingdom, could not stop the evil which might grow within the kingdom, from growing. Thus the evil son grew more evil each day. He could not appreciate the beauty that was around him. He was never happy and envied his brother's happiness. Finally, the evil son decided that he alone should rule the kingdom after their father died, and he plotted against his older brother.

When news of the plot reached the king, he realized that his evil son would never learn to be good within the kingdom. So he sent him away, outside the cloud of protection. Try as he might, the evil son could not reenter the kingdom, because the cloud became a solid wall in front of him.

The evil son went to live in a distant land. Through violence and theft he became very powerful. One day a report came to the king that this evil son was organizing an army to overthrow him and take the kingdom for himself.

The king knew the evil son could never enter the kingdom with soldiers. The cloud would protect them. But he missed his son, and hoped that perhaps the young man might change his evil ways.

"There must be a way we can transform the evil in my son's heart," the king said before his chief minister.

The chief minister thought a while and said, "Send your good son out to him."

"He will be in danger," protested the king.

"Give him your royal scepter," said the minister. "It will protect him."

The king called for the good son and explained his mission. He was to travel to the land of his evil brother and try to bring him home.

"But father," said the good son, "as soon as he sees me, he will want to kill me."

"The scepter will protect you," said the king.

The good son left the palace and went to the land of his brother. The people there made fun of him. They said he was a weak prince and his older brother would one day be king. He was arrested and taken to a dungeon beneath his brother's palace. It was dark and wet and filled with crawling creatures. All he was fed was hard bread and water, and he feared he'd be forgotten there forever.

Then one day a loud noise was heard in the dungeon. A troop of soldiers marched down the stone tunnels and stopped in front of his cell. They opened the gate and said, "We are here to take you to be tried for crimes against your brother."

The good son was taken to a great courtroom. There sat his brother on a high platform. "Why did you come to my land?" he shouted.

"Our father sent me."

"And why did our father send you?"

"To bring you back to the Kingdom of Light."

"Hah!" cried the evil son disdainfully. "Then our father has sent you on a fool's errand. And in our land fools have no place. Prepare yourself brother, for today will be your last day on earth."

"Then you shall never know the secret of the scepter," said the good son.

The evil son thought for a minute. Then he had a guard bring him the scepter. Try as he might he could see no magic symbols or hidden compartments in the scepter. In disgust, he threw it at his brother.

*Varoom!* A cloud appeared in front of the good brother. It covered him completely. Then the walls began to shake and the ceiling came down burying everyone in the chamber but the good brother and his evil sibling.

A voice spoke.

"That which is ordained cannot be changed. You have sought to destroy the good and so you will be destroyed.

You have defiled my scepter and my land. And you have poisoned your own soul.

"Till you purify that which you have profaned, you will never have peace again."

The smoke cleared and the two brothers faced each other. The evil brother had terror in his eyes. The good brother took pity on him.

"How will I purify myself?" the evil brother pleaded.

"I will show you how," answered the good brother. "You must come back with me. Back to our father."

So they went back to the magical kingdom. But the evil son could not get into the kingdom. Try as he might, the cloud would not let him in. His father, the king, came out to console him, to help him purify himself, but still he could not get in. For him, the cloud continued to be a solid wall.

The evil son put on sackcloth and fasted for days on end. Finally, he was close to death.

And still the cloud barred his entrance into his father's kingdom.

Finally, the good son came to his brother. "I thought that your acts of regret and repentance would help you come back to us, but I see it is not so. Do not lose hope, however, I have a plan."

Without hesitation, the good son picked up his weaker younger brother and clasped him to his chest. He rushed toward the cloud which now parted and let them both in.

Everyone in the Kingdom of Light cheered as the good son came through the cloud and fell into the open arms of the waiting crowd. Suddenly, the evil son felt his

*Without hesitation, the good son picked up his weaker younger brother and clasped him to his chest. He rushed toward the cloud which now parted and let them both in.*

strength return. He got up and for the first time saw the beauty that was part of his heritage. He bowed deeply to his father.

The father extended his hands to his sons and said:

"You have both learned something this land cannot teach you. That goodness must not sit quietly behind a cloud, indifferent to the outside world. Goodness must seek out and help the truly repentant cross the barriers of evil every man creates for himself. Let that be your legacy, and may you both rule this kingdom in peace."

Saba fell silent. He stared at the Sabbath candles.

Eli felt that the battle between the good son and the bad son was the battle between his grandfather and him against Jaktabar. But why does the good son help the bad son? And how could they possibly make Jaktabar overcome his own barriers?

"Wait and see," his grandfather suddenly said to no one in particular.

But Eli knew he was talking to him.

Chapter 11

# Map of the Treasure

The evening ended and the guests left. Eli went to sleep on the couch. Rabbi Mordechai told him they would have to wake up very early to prepare for the Sabbath morning prayers.

Several hours later Eli heard a voice and awoke. Saba was standing over him in his white robe. "Come," he said. "It is time."

Eli pulled on his clothes and followed him out the door. Glancing at his watch he saw that it was two in the morning. He had never gotten up so early.

The night was cool and clear. Saba led Eli up several narrow alleys with hidden entrances and tiny staircases that never seemed to end. Finally they came to the old synagogue of Rabbi Ya'acov Abuhav. To Eli's surprise, the room was filled with swaying old men who rose from their seats when Saba entered. He took a chair at the head of the main table and the men went back to their holy books, reading out loud and swaying to a hidden rhythm. Saba listened but said nothing. When a clash of opinions broke out between two sages, they would turn to him. Then, without looking at any books, Saba would elaborate both sides of the argument, arriving at a solution that seemed to satisfy both men. And so the learning continued into the early morning.

Eli was fascinated. He understood little of what the sages were saying, but felt he was learning just by looking at their faces. Slowly Eli recognized a few men he had seen in town. One operated a grocery and another repaired radios. He had assumed they were simple people and not very learned, but here they were, on the Sabbath, studying the intricacies of Jewish Law and mysticism.

After an hour Eli grew tired and his eyes became heavy, but he was afraid to sleep. He took out his Bible and turned to Kings I and reread the story of Saul and the Witch of Endor. For the first time he understood why Saul wanted to know his fate. It wasn't that the king was afraid of dying, he just wanted to know that his children would live on after him and rule the kingdom. He wanted that feeling of continuity. The very continuity that Eli was feeling now with Saba. This was what really counted. This knowledge made Eli smile as he found himself swaying gently to the beat of his own chant. After a while, he felt himself nodding off. The Hebrew words on the page blurred. He leaned against his grandfather and fell asleep.

The rest of the Sabbath passed quickly. The morning prayers, the festive meal, the songs and stories, the afternoon nap, the third meal of the Sabbath, more songs and stories and words of wisdom. It made Eli feel as though he had taken a journey into another world, another dimension.

This is what it must be like in heaven, he thought. The people work all week just for the sake of the Sabbath. It was so different back home, everyone was so involved in the physical world, they didn't have enough time to really experience the Sabbath.

When he told his grandfather how he felt, his Saba said:

"A Jew who enjoys his Sabbath has tasted one-sixtieth of the World to Come."

By the evening prayers, when the sun had disappeared beyond Mt. Meron, Eli felt sorry the day of rest was almost over.

After *Havdallah*, the blessings that ended the Sabbath, Saba lit a tall candle, opened an old wooden case and drew out an instrument that looked like a cross between a flute and a clarinet. He began playing a soft melody. It was a haunting tune that gathered momentum as he swayed back and forth, his fingers floating over the holes. Then, with a leap from his chair, he played a quick Middle Eastern tune similar to the one Eli had heard on the tape player in Moshe's taxi. He danced a little jig as he played and Eli joined the dance. The sadness of the Sabbath's passing lifted. A new week had begun.

When Saba had caught his breath, he said, "Now we can begin the new week with hope and joy. Here, sit beside me."

Eli drew a chair up to the desk while Saba took out

the old yellowed envelope which contained Rabbi Ya'acov's documents.

One of the papers was a crude hand-drawn map. It showed a floor-plan of the room under the old house. Saba read the notes on the map in Hebrew. Eli looked over the diagram to see how it matched his memory of the room he had entered. On the map there was a corridor off the main room that he had not seen when he was in the ruins.

"This wasn't down there," he said to Saba.

The old man examined the document. "Are you sure?" he asked. "Perhaps it was hidden by fallen stones. Many earthquakes have hit this area since the time of Rabbi Ya'acov."

"Maybe someone closed it up or built on it."

Saba listened but did not answer. He was thinking of something else.

"Perhaps this corridor is at an even deeper level," he said, "and Rabbi Ya'acov drew it as if it were on the same level."

Eli hadn't thought of that.

"You will have to find the corridor," Saba said. "And at the end is the spot where the treasure is hidden. He writes that it is behind a stone at the base of the western wall. Search for a loose stone near the floor."

Eli shrank in his chair.

"I knew I'd have to go down there again," he muttered softly.

"You don't want to?" Saba asked.

"It's not that I don't want to," the boy said. "It's just

that it's kind of spooky."

Saba's brow creased in concern. "You don't have to go," he said.

"I do have to go," said Eli. "It's part of our inheritance, isn't it? From Rabbi Ya'acov?"

Saba nodded very slowly, examining the boy's face.

"Yes," he said. "It's from Rabbi Ya'acov. He has indicated here," he held up a sheet of writing, "certain signs and secrets we can use in our efforts against Jaktabar." He scanned one particular symbol that had ancient Hebrew writing all around it. "There is even a reference to you."

"To me? Where?" Eli sprang back to life.

"Here. It says that someone in the fourth generation will come from far away to help remove the curse. Who else could it be?"

Eli shivered. He felt he had little control over his life. Some powerful mystical force was orchestrating events.

Well, I suppose that settles it," he said with renewed conviction. "Now I *have* to go down there."

"But you still have a choice," Saba cautioned.

"Not if I'm the fourth generation, I don't," Eli announced, almost defiantly.

Saba touched his shoulder, and smiled.

## Chapter 12
# Bats!

The next morning Eli once again slung the canvas bag over his shoulder and headed for the house of the three sisters. He found them chattering excitedly. He couldn't hear what they were saying, but he sensed that Saba's blessing was beginning to have an effect. The eldest sister seemed to know he was coming and led him down to the cellar. She got out the rope again.

This time Eli lowered himself into the hole with more confidence. At the bottom he passed through the stone-filled archway and entered the ruins of Rabbi Ya'acov's house. Shining the flashlight around the room, he saw everything was the same as before except...

A half-burnt candle stood on the desktop. He touched the wick and a speck of charcoal crushed onto his finger-tip. Someone had been here after his last visit.

Eli suddenly felt he was being watched. Slowly, he turned to check the rest of the dark musty room, but it was just as he remembered it.

He quickly went back to the shaft he had climbed down and called up to the sisters. No answer. He called again, raising his voice, but there was still no answer. Could they have left him alone down there and gone off? He was about to start climbing up the well when the eldest sister answered.

"Has anyone been down here besides me?" Eli called up.

There was a brief silence, then the voice came down the dark shaft, "I don't think so."

"Are you sure?" he cried.

"A worker came to the house, maybe he went down?" she said.

"What kind of worker?"

"What kind? I don't know. I wasn't here. My sister was here."

"Ask her."

There was a long pause and then she returned.

"She says she thinks he was from the village. He had said he was sent by your Saba to check some damage to the well."

Eli felt a chill in his bones. Jaktabar must have sent him to find the treasure and maybe to curse the house again. There was no time to lose. He had to find the treasure, now. Quickly, he returned to the main room.

At a small archway at the far end of the room, he pushed open a tiny door. It looked like no more than a closet. The hinges were rusty and the door seemed stuck. Pressing his foot against the wall and pushing with all his strength, Eli felt the wooden frame crack. Another mighty push and the door broke loose, and before he knew it, Eli went lunging into the darkness.

He landed with a thud and found himself in a short corridor with a low ceiling. This led to a narrow staircase which dropped almost straight down into a cellar. Bending over, he carefully climbed down the stairs. When he reached the bottom, the flashlight illuminated another barren room and what he thought was the beginning of another staircase. Eli remembered seeing a painting of a staircase leading to another staircase which led to another staircase which seemed to go on forever.

I never thought I would actually be living that painting, he thought. But then he realized the other "staircase" was just an illusion, a shadow caught by his flashlight. This was a dead end. There was no way out except to retrace his steps.

Eli sensed, more than felt, something above him. He raised the flashlight's beam and saw that the room was filled with bats! They were hanging upside down along the ceiling, still as statues. Eli gasped in fear. There were hundreds of them, all huddled together. But they didn't move. He took a closer look and then touched one of the bats with his flashlight. Nothing. He touched it harder, and a bat fell to the floor dead.

All the bats were dead. What could have killed them like that? Then he remembered Saba talking about earthquakes. If there had been an earthquake, poisonous gases might have seeped into the room and killed all the bats as they slept.

But how did the bats get into the room in the first

*Eli sensed, more than felt, something above him. He raised the flashlight's beam and saw that the room was filled with bats!*

place? They certainly did not come in through the sisters' house. That must mean there is another opening into the room. Another corridor must be hidden somewhere in this room. Perhaps this was the missing corridor on the map!

Eli forgot his fear as he shone the flashlight across the room. There! To the right of him was a crack that started from the top of the wall and ended about a foot above the ground. The crack and the wall ended together. Below them was empty space. Just enough space for Eli to crawl through.

He wiggled his way into another corridor. He was dusting himself off when he heard something that made him freeze. At the end of the corridor, out of the blackness, he heard the grunts and groans of men hard at work.

## Chapter 13
# Death Grip

Eli stood perfectly still. Was the corridor the path to the outside? Had he gone through all this just to find himself back in front of the sisters' house?

He slowly made his way down the corridor. At first his own breathing was louder and more distinct than the voices of the men. As he continued walking, he heard a new sound, the ping of shovels and picks against stone. He still wasn't sure where the sound was coming from. He followed the corridor as it turned sharply right. Suddenly, it ended at a damp, moldy wall. He put his ear to the wall and heard the men on the other side. They were speaking Arabic.

Jaktabar's men!

This must be the wall Saba had pointed to on Rabbi Ya'acov's map. The Arabs must know this also. But why are they digging toward me? Almost as he thought it, the answer came to him. They think the treasure is in here!

Eli pointed the flashlight up and saw a shaft like the

one he had climbed down. This was where the bats must have come from. Then he turned the flashlight back to the wall. He began examining the stones. Before long he noticed a stone that had been cut differently than the others. It was an almost perfect square and so smooth it was obvious someone had spent a long time cutting it. He took a short pickaxe from his canvas bag and tried to pry the stone loose. It moved! Carefully, but quickly, Eli edged the stone out. He lifted it, expecting to bend under its weight, but he found it weighed very little. He put it on the floor and immediately realized why it had been so light. The stone's center had been hollowed out. Inside, under an old rag, lay a small metal box. Rabbi Ya'acov's treasure! He lifted up the box and shook it as he held it to his ear. He heard a crash. But it wasn't the box. A stone had fallen from the wall. The Arab workers had broken through!

A voice shouted and then a head appeared through the small opening. Without thinking Eli picked up the fallen stone and rushed to push it back into the wall. But as he got close to the wall a hand shot through the opening and grabbed his hand in a vice-like grip.

"Yow!" he yelled, dropping the stone. On the other side of the wall, the Arab screamed to his companions to work fast to finish opening the wall. The powerful hand continued to hold Eli flush against the cold stones.

Eli dropped the treasure and, using his free hand, pushed with all his strength against the wall. He felt his arm being pulled out of its socket. Groaning from the exertion and the pain, he pushed his knees up against the wall and slowly dragged his hand back through the hole. He lifted the pickaxe with his free arm and, as the man's fingers came through the hole he crashed the pickaxe down, hard. A bloodcurdling yell came from the Arab as he let go. Eli could see blood dripping onto the stones.

Eli fell to the floor, the pain in his arm was excruciating. The men on the other side redoubled their efforts to break down the wall and stones started falling down all around him.

He couldn't move. He knew when they came through they would kill him.

Then, as the first Arab began to climb through the wall, a rumbling rose up from the center of the earth. The walls of the corridor began to shake and crumble. The ground trembled and pieces of rotten wood from the shaft above began to rain down.

Earthquake!

## Chapter 14

# Captured by the Sorcerer

Eli woke up to find Saba looking at him. A smile slowly spread across his face as Eli opened his eyes, wide with disbelief.

"Stay still," Saba commanded. "Nothing is broken, but the doctor said you should not move around until after he has had a chance to examine you."

Eli didn't remember anything from the moment the ground began to tremble.

"I will answer all your questions," Saba said. "Jaktabar's men *were* trying to kill you. But God works in His own way, and two of them died in the earthquake. Also, the treasure was recovered when you were taken out of the corridor. We sent down a search party and they were able to bring you out on a stretcher. Don't worry, the treasure is in our house, well hidden. You will see it later. The house of the three sisters was not damaged badly and although everyone in town was frightened, no one else was harmed. A true miracle, blessed be His Name, that the earthquake began and ended in the corridor you discovered. I think it is time to call the doctor."

The doctor gave Eli a clean bill of health. The three sisters came and they thanked Eli and Saba over and over. Eli wasn't quite sure for what.

"The eldest has been betrothed," Saba said, once again reading Eli's mind. "And the middle sister has begun keeping company with one of the local rabbi's sons, a *talmid chacham*, a wise young man. But there is still the matter of the youngest sister..." From the twinkle in Saba's eye, Eli was able to read Saba's mind, but he was in no hurry to jump from his Bar Mitzvah to the wedding canopy.

Eli rested for a few days, spending his time reading and relaxing. Twice he asked to see the inheritance, but his grandfather put him off each time. Finally, one afternoon, Saba came to him and said:

"We are almost there, Eli. Soon you will know a small part of your destiny. Be patient. The inheritance of Rabbi Ya'acov will be yours very soon."

Eli felt good knowing his grandfather would soon reveal the treasure he had come 6,000 miles and endured some hair-raising adventures, to see.

He felt strong enough to take a walk. It was beautiful outside, and he hated being cooped up. So, assuring his grandfather he would not stray far, Eli left the house, deep in thought, wondering what the treasure could be and what he would do with it.

A white van followed Eli down the street. Eli barely noticed when the van pulled up beside him. The driver smiled, revealing a large golden tooth. Eli blinked, wondering why the driver was smiling at him. Just then the side door of the van banged open and two men jumped out. One brandished an automatic weapon, the other a short rope. They grabbed him before he knew what had happened and threw him into the back of the van. In seconds he was blindfolded and his hands tied tightly and roughly behind his back. All the while, his kidnappers kept shouting at him in Arabic.

After about 20 minutes the van made a sharp turn and slowed. Someone carried Eli into a house, up a flight of steps and dropped him into a chair in a cool, quiet room. He smelled something like ashes mixed with spices. Suddenly, Eli's blindfold was removed.

He looked up, squinting in the bright light, to see Jaktabar himself standing over him, his black kaftan like a dark cloud filling the tiny room.

"So this is the fourth generation I was warned about! Ha! Ha! Ha! If only all my enemies were so...little. I'm sure you know why you were brought here. We want the treasure of Rabbi Ya'acov that was hidden in the house of Jaktabar! My house. It is mine! Your grandfather should have known better than to bring you into our personal battle. What happens to you will be on his head!" He took a chair and sat facing Eli. The guard stood behind him, at attention, his rifle pointing at the ceiling.

Without warning, Jaktabar swung an open hand and struck Eli across the face, knocking him to the floor. Jaktabar ordered the guard to put Eli back on the chair.

Still bound with ropes, the boy raised himself to his knees and was placed on the chair.

"That is to remind you who owns you now, little dog," Jaktabar snarled.

"Saba will come soon," Eli whispered.

"Yes, he will," shouted Jaktabar. "With Rabbi Ya'acov's treasure in hand. I have sent your grandfather a message telling him I will trade you for the treasure. Your grandfather will not betray you. He will give up the treasure because he is old and weak and does not deserve to use its hidden powers. "As for you," he hissed, leaning a few inches from Eli's face, "if you are not careful, your mouth will dig your grave."

## Chapter 15

# "Bow Down!"

Several hours later, a guard brought Eli a plate of pita bread, a basin and a vessel of water. The guard untied his hands and feet, and Eli washed for bread and made the appropriate blessings. He was surprised his captors knew and respected his religious customs by bringing him water to wash.

The guard looked at him with dark suspicion.

"Do Muslims wash before eating bread?" Eli asked in Hebrew.

The guard grunted.

"There is an impure spirit on the hands," he told the man. "We wash to remove the impurity."

The guard shouted in Arabic to be quiet.

Eli saw the guard was not anxious to make friends, so he continued with his meal.

He ate silently and then recited the Blessing After Meals. Eli couldn't help but feel that at a time like this prayers took on a deeper, more spiritual meaning, even prayers he had taken for granted. The guard removed the plate and basin and left them outside the door. Eli began to nod off, but was careful not to fall off the chair.

He awoke in pain a few hours later. Angry shouts came from outside the room. It sounded like Jaktabar giving orders to his men. Footsteps pounded on the stones and up the stairs. In a moment, the door to the room was thrown open, and a guard came in. Eli assumed Saba had come, brought the treasure and made the transaction with Jaktabar. In a matter of moments he would be free.

Then he heard a slow rhythmic climb up the stairway outside the room. He had heard these footsteps in Saba's house when his grandfather went about his morning routine. This time the steps were slower. Eli heard strained breathing. Then a voice.

"Eli, I am here."

Saba entered, bent over, leaning on a wooden cane. He was followed by a second guard with a rifle.

"Shalom Aleichem," Saba said.

Eli started to answer him, but Saba warned, "Quiet. Say nothing now."

Eli found it difficult to be silent. "I knew you'd come, Saba," he whispered. "I knew you'd make the trade. I never thought for a moment —"

Saba's grim look made Eli stop in mid-sentence. Something was wrong, terribly wrong.

Suddenly Jaktabar entered the room, pushing the guard out of his way.

"You thought?" the sorcerer bellowed. "What is this

thought! I have donkeys with more thoughts than you Americans. The famous wisdom of your family," he said glaring at Saba, "must be running dry."

Eli felt like a soldier whose general has surrendered just as the battle was about to be won.

One of the guards brought a chair for Saba. Jaktabar ordered both guards to leave the room. Then Jaktabar began pacing around the low-ceilinged room. He was a tall thin man in his sixties with a thin, scraggly beard, uneven blackened teeth offset with several gold caps, and a twitch in his left eye which gave Eli the impression he was winking, perhaps to some invisible being or demon.

Jaktabar inhaled with deep satisfaction, swelling his chest like some beast who has just conquered his prey.

"Ah, if only my father could see this great moment, the son of Rabbi Ya'acov in the hands of the son of Mufti Jaktabar. I would keep you here a long time, rabbi, merely to prolong this moment. But since I now have the secrets of Rabbi Ya'acov, thanks to our guest from America, I'm afraid I won't be able to indulge myself in this pleasure." He paused, standing before Saba. "But there is one pleasure I will not deny myself," he said. "Having you, great rabbi, bow down before me, your new master."

Saba's lips were a straight unswerving line.

"Bow!" ordered Jaktabar. "Bow to me, your new master!"

Saba just gazed at Jaktabar calmly. "You know I cannot. I'll give my life first. And so will my grandson."

Eli's stomach twisted into a knot. It had not occurred

to him that he would have to make such a choice.

"Will he?" said Jaktabar, sensing Eli's nervousness. "Are you so sure?"

He stepped over to Eli. A slow trickle of sweat dripped down the boy's back.

"Bow down!" Jaktabar commanded.

Eli sat frozen.

"Bow down!" He slapped him, even harder than before. Eli fell to the floor, landing with a thud on his side.

Saba jumped up, waving his cane at Jaktabar. The sorcerer wheeled about and knocked the cane from the old man's hand.

Eli tried to get up, making sure not to be caught in a bowing position, but Jaktabar put his foot on his back and pushed him down. "Stupid American, bow down. Bow to your master."

Eli pursed his lips tightly. He couldn't move.

"Say this," Jaktabar demanded. "Allah is the master of life and death, Jaktabar is His Prophet."

"God is the master of life and death," said Eli.

Jaktabar kicked him and turned furiously to Saba.

"I am tired of your games," he sneered at Rabbi Mordechai. "With the treasure in my hands I will have all the wealth and power I need to make these lands mine again. Then I will not be so polite about asking you and your dog to bow down."

Abruptly, Jaktabar left, slamming the door behind him.

When he was sure the evil sorcerer was gone, Eli picked himself up. He felt bruised everywhere.

"Are you badly hurt?" asked Saba.

"No," Eli said hoarsely. "I'm just glad he didn't touch you."

"Each time he hit you," Saba said, a strange anger burning in his eyes, "he touched me. Rest assured, he will have his due, very soon."

"But what happened, Saba?" Eli asked, bewildered. "I thought it would be a simple switch. You give him the treasure and he lets me free."

"Nothing in our battle with the Other Side is simple," Saba answered.

"So he just tricked you?"

Saba smiled. "Perhaps."

"But I thought there would be an exchange —"

"I did not want an exchange," said Saba. "I will not give away Rabbi Ya'acov's inheritance to that madman. As always, in this world, to gain something we must first give something. Today we have given. Tomorrow we will see."

"I don't understand."

"That is the beginning of knowledge," said Rabbi Mordechai. Then he became more serious. "The next step will soon be clear."

*"Bow down!" Jaktabar commanded.*

## Chapter 16

# A Snake in the Garden

Saba, are you awake," whispered Eli in the darkness. He didn't know how long he had been asleep.

"Yes," Rabbi Mordechai answered.

"The guard is sleeping," Eli said. "We could try to slip by him."

"Not now," he said.

"But it would be easy," Eli persisted.

"It is not the time," Saba repeated.

"Why not?" Eli pleaded. "He may come back and force us to bow down."

"I will tell you a story," Saba intoned, starting to gently sway back and forth. "There was once a king who had a beautiful garden where he would walk with his son. One day they came upon a snake. The king commanded his son to get the snake out of the garden. But the prince said, 'How can I? The snake is deadly and he's gone into his hole.' 'Find a way to get him out of the hole,' said the king, 'Or the garden will never be safe.' The prince thought for a long time. If he reached blindly into the hole, he would be bitten and die. If he waited outside the hole, the snake would see him and never come out, or perhaps escape when the prince was asleep. Finally, the king's son decided to dig his own hole next to the snake's. He would enter the snake's lair by surprise, and kill him. Then the garden would be safe forever. And that is exactly what happened."

Eli thought a while, then whispered, "I think I understand. We are in our hole next to the snake. In a moment we will spring and kill him. Only," Eli looked a little sheepish, as though he really didn't want to continue the analogy. "Only I think the snake knows where we are and may spring on us first."

"Perhaps," came the enigmatic answer. "But remember, the master often believes he controls the servant only to find out that the clever servant is really *his* master."

"But —"

Suddenly the guard let out a loud snore and startled himself awake. His black eyes burned with fear, as though he had just been awakened from a terrible nightmare.

Saba took a cigarette from his pocket and offered it to the guard.

Where did Saba get a cigarette from, wondered Eli. He doesn't smoke.

The guard warily accepted the cigarette, lit it and inhaled.

"Ah, American. Very good." He relished every drag,

the glowing tip dancing in the dark like a firefly.

Saba spoke in Arabic and soon the guard and Saba were deep in conversation. Handing the pack of cigarettes to the guard, Saba gestured for him to keep them. Eli could see the guard smile behind the glow of the ash. Saba had made a friend. They spoke a while longer, in a friendly tone.

"What're you talking about?" Eli whispered, when Saba turned back from the guard.

"Don't whisper," Saba said. "It'll make him suspicious.

"I asked about his wife and children, and gave them a blessing. He says his master has been very nervous lately. Short tempered and mean. All the men are very afraid of him."

A little later, before dawn broke, the sound of Moslem morning prayers wafted through the village.

Saba asked for water to wash their hands and began to recite his morning prayers.

Then Saba recited verses by heart and asked Eli to repeat after him. They spent the morning this way, covering many passages of the Torah and the Prophets. When Eli had a question, Saba would explain the details and ask him to repeat the explanation. The guard was intrigued with the dialogue between grandfather and grandson.

Suddenly footsteps pounded up the stairs. The guard leaped up and stood menacingly above them. The door swung open and Jaktabar entered.

"I had a strange dream last night," he blurted out, without introduction, glaring at Rabbi Mordechai. He began at once pacing the small room and dismissed the guard with a wave of his hand. The guard looked relieved.

"I saw fish swimming in a fountain and I was trying to catch one in my net, but each time I caught him I would look down and he would be gone, swimming in the fountain again."

Saba smiled. "Some of our sages teach that dreams are meaningless and others say they follow the word of the interpreter. Still others say they are an aspect of prophecy."

Jaktabar's eyes burned like coals. "Games again? You want to play games?" he shouted. "Ahmed!" He hollered and the guard returned.

The sorcerer ordered the guard to strike Saba, but the guard hesitated. Ahmed stared into Saba's eyes. He raised his hand, but instead of bringing it down he began to tremble.

"You should hit me," Saba said in Arabic. But the guard just continued to tremble until it looked like he might come apart.

Jaktabar grabbed the guard and threw him out the door, down the steps. Furious, he stalked back into the room.

"Your dream is this," Saba suddenly announced. "We are the fish and while you may capture us, you cannot hold us, even when we are in your net. You think you have us, but we are part of the fountain, the waters of the Living Torah."

"The holy Koran contains all the secrets of the Universe," Jaktabar intoned, and then quoted a verse from memory.

Saba smiled and was silent.

"Very well," said Jaktabar. "Dreams are only dreams. But this," he took a dagger from the folds of his kaftan, "this is not a dream." He stepped toward Eli and placed the cold blade of the knife against his neck. "Now," Jaktabar said to Rabbi Mordechai, "kneel down to me, or there will be a fountain, a fountain of blood, and it will not be a dream but a nightmare."

Chapter 17

# Magical Flower

Eli sat trembling. The knife nicked his skin and a red rivulet raced down his neck. He didn't feel a thing. He was too afraid to think or feel.

"Kneel down!" Jaktabar commanded. "Kneel, false prophet, or you will see how easy it is to catch and kill a small fish."

Saba was unmoving. His eyes closed and he began rocking again. Jaktabar looked ready to carry out his threat. Eli felt his heart pumping faster and faster.

Suddenly, a sonic boom broke the tension. It was an Israeli jet heading north to some secret rendezvous. But for Jaktabar, it was as though heaven had spoken to him. His features softened, dramatically. He eased the pressure on his knife and Eli looked up at him. For a split second Eli could have sworn Jaktabar looked very much like...Rabbi Mordechai.

Images of the Sabbath story that Saba had told sailed through his mind. One brother an outcast, the other wanting to help him but not knowing how, until he takes him up like a child and carries him to safety inside the cloud. Was this the fate of these two leaders? Was Jaktabar going to ask for Saba to help him cross over, return to...the Kingdom of Light? Was this the moment?

But the moment passed and the sorcerer smiled his terrible smile.

"You are stubborn," he admitted to Rabbi Mordechai, as he released his grip on Eli entirely. "Being a follower of Islam and a man of God, I appreciate that. We also bow to Allah and no other."

"Then why do you use the magic of the Other Side?" asked Saba, opening his eyes and speaking softly, as though to a loved one.

"The ways of Allah are hidden," the sorcerer whispered, echoing words Rabbi Mordechai had said a million times before.

Jaktabar returned the dagger to its sheath in his kaftan, and abruptly left.

A short while later they heard scuffling downstairs and then one short cry that faded into a whimper. Saba closed his eyes and said a prayer. Eli wondered what had happened, but before he could ask, the door opened. A new guard came in and sat cross-legged on the floor.

Later that afternoon, Saba asked permission to walk outside for the afternoon prayer. Jaktabar was away, but the guard called in two other Arabs to accompany Rabbi Mordechai outside. Eli wanted to go, too, but the guard adamantly refused.

"Don't worry," Saba told him, "I'll be back soon."

An hour later he returned, looking pleased.

"God is very good," he said, barely containing his excitement. He removed a plant from his pocket. "He helped me find this very special flower."

Eli had no idea why this flower was so special, or what Saba intended to do with it, but when the door opened and Jaktabar came in, his grandfather quickly stuffed the flower back into his pocket.

"I have had another dream," Jaktabar announced.

"Where is the guard who was here before?" Saba asked, obviously angry. The battle between them was beginning anew.

"He has gone," answered the sorcerer.

"Is that how you reward your servants?" Saba exclaimed, raising his voice. "Is that how you praise Allah, by murdering your servant? I do not wish to hear your dreams. You dream the dreams of the dead."

Jaktabar glared at him. "So be it. My dream was of you. If I dreamed the dreams of the dead then you will die with me, old man."

"I will die," Saba told him. "But not with you. Never with you."

"I believe that destroying an infidel, even if in the process I, too, am destroyed, will gain me entry to the gates of Heaven," Jaktabar said, ignoring Rabbi Mordechai's remarks. "And you believe that by dying for your belief, you enter the gates of Heaven. So perhaps we shall both become martyrs very soon," he sneered.

"You have spoken with the dead," Saba said.

For a moment Jaktabar lost all color in his face.

"You have seen the worlds of angels and souls. You know how to manipulate the forces of creation. So let me ask you: Knowing all you know and having seen all you have seen, if you were the Master of the World would you bring a murderer into your palace of holiness?

"You know the answer, Jaktabar. And yet you still prefer falsehood and murder. You hide from the Light and from the Truth."

"The Truth? What Truth?" Jaktabar growled.

"That you are the slave of your power. You do not act, you are acted upon by the evil in your heart. You are its puppet. You did not kill that guard. The evil master who rules your heart killed him. And as for your dream, I know the fountain of fire you were swimming in. And yes, it was me standing at the edge with a rope, a rope that I tried again and again to reach you with. Shall I interpret all this for you Jaktabar?"

Jaktabar turned white, suddenly looking old and frail. His blazing eyes faded like dying embers. He pulled his beard in agitation.

"How-How did you know?"

It was Saba's turn to laugh.

"How did you know?" Jaktabar commanded. The laughter only made him angrier. "You mock me! But I can still kill you. I can still cut off your head and hang you in the street like a thief. How did you know?" he screamed.

"Jaktabar," Saba said, almost in a whisper. "You have no need to be afraid of us."

"Afraid of you! May Allah cut me down if I am afraid

of you!"

"We shall see," said Saba. He closed his eyes, a sign that the time for talking had passed.

"You still have not told me how you knew my dream," shouted Jaktabar, grabbing Rabbi Mordechai's coat. But Saba remained immobile.

"Perhaps the little one knows," said the sorcerer, turning to Eli. "How did your grandfather know my dream?"

Eli remembered his own dream, of the massacre in Tzfat, and how Saba had talked about the mind like a movie projector of dreams.

"Maybe he put it there," Eli blurted out, without really knowing why.

Jaktabar looked at him and then at Saba. He jumped up, knocking over his chair. "Fools!" he cried, the color returning to his face. He stormed out of the room, slamming the door so hard that loose plaster fell from the wall.

That night, as the guard sat sleeping, Eli saw Saba pressing something in his coat pocket. It looked like he was crushing something. After a while, he handed Eli a handful of powder and said, "Take this downstairs and put it in the hookah where they smoke their tobacco."

"What is it?" asked Eli.

"The special flower I found."

"What about Jaktabar?"

"There is no need to worry about him right now. Move quickly and quietly."

Eli started for the door, then turned back.

"Saba, how do you know he went out?"

Rabbi Mordechai smiled. "You still need to ask?" he said.

Chapter 18
# The Chest of Bones

Eli bumped his head on the staircase's low ceiling, smothering a cry by biting his lip. Passing along a corridor, he smelled something strange coming from a room on his left. The smell reminded him of the biology lab in school. He passed the room and stood in front of a large living room. He took one step inside and his heart skipped a beat. Despite the darkness he could make out someone sleeping on the couch. Beside the sleeping form, on a low table, stood the hookah — its long smoking cord coiled like a snake around the pipe's glass stem. A lump of ash rested on the pipe's bowl where Eli was supposed to sprinkle the powder. Hoping his pounding heart would not rouse the guard, he sprinkled the powder onto the ash and backed away from the table. Suddenly, headlights pulled up to the front window and voices sounded outside the door.

Eli panicked and backed into a coat rack, getting tangled up in an old kaftan and turban which had fallen on him. A key turned in the front door, and Eli scrambled out of the living room and into the nearest doorway, the strange clothes partially wrapped around his head and shoulders. Hearing Jaktabar shout at the sleeping guard, Eli held his breath. He had bolted into the room with the lab odor. As he looked around, he realized this was indeed some sort of laboratory.

The walls were covered with shelves of glass jars. Inside were rats' heads and feet, snake skins, bird wings and organs of various animals. One section seemed to be devoted to specimens of human hair and long fingernails. In this section stood a jar that held two large white eyeballs, their pupils dilated, floating in a formaldehyde solution. A sickening feeling rose in Eli's stomach. He felt the eyeballs staring at him and abruptly turned away. "My God," he mumbled, "this must be where Jaktabar performs black magic."

As he continued scanning the room he spotted the metal treasure box of Rabbi Ya'acov on Jaktabar's desk.

Suddenly the door to the lab burst open and Eli darted under a sheet hung over a long table. Slowly he raised his head and then froze. Hanging off the table's edge just above him was a stiff dark hand.

The light switched on and Eli heard Jaktabar enter the room with someone behind him. They would surely find him now. But the sorcerer and his men did not approach the table. He peeked out behind the sheet and saw that Jaktabar was handling the treasure box, looking for some secret opening. Afraid to be seen, Eli ducked his head back beneath the table. He crawled toward the back of the table, so he would be safely hidden, and bumped into a large chest.

Actually, it looked more like a coffin than a chest. Lifting the lid a little, Eli saw a mass of bones. Besides the bones was a map of Israel. There were red circles drawn around a number of areas. Eli gasped. In a flash, he realized what was happening. The sorcerer had collected these bones and was going to put them in all the water stations and reservoirs in Israel!

Jaktabar shouted something in Arabic. Eli peered out from underneath the table and saw the sorcerer reading a document he had obviously found in the treasure box. Then he raised his head and marched straight toward Eli.

They're coming for the box, he realized. Eli quickly lifted the lid high enough so he could squeeze inside. An instant later, the men reached under the table and slid the box out.

He heard the men groan as they lifted him and the box. The lid of the box rattled up and down as they walked and he was sure they would see him. But, before long they lowered the box to the ground near the side of the house and were called away.

When he was sure they were gone, Eli pushed the lid up a crack and saw two guards standing on the front porch, rifles on their hips. The men were facing away from him. Could he dash around the back of the house without their seeing him? It was his only chance. He raised the lid inch by inch then rolled out of the box. Like a commando, he wiggled his body toward the house. A Cedar tree rose near an exterior wall, passing the window where he was sure Saba was waiting for him. Eli had never climbed a Cedar before. As he pulled himself up he found that the bark fell away in his hands, making him lose his grip. Finally, in desperation, he hugged the tree, climbing up like a caterpillar, inch by inch. After a long time he reached his room. Carefully, he stepped through the open window and was pulled down by an unseen hand just as he was about to lower himself to the floor.

"Feeling restless, little American?" Jaktabar asked, holding Eli by his shirt. The lights went on and Eli saw his grandfather at the other end of the room, sitting, Indian style, on the floor. "Perhaps you would like to come with us tonight?" the sorcerer suggested.

"Where are you going?"

"I think you know where I'm going," Jaktabar stated. "Did you think I would not know what goes on in my own room? Did you have a nice climb?" he asked, mockingly.

Eli realized that Jaktabar had just been playing with him. There was nothing left to lose.

"If you curse all the waters of Israel," Eli burst out, "what will you and your people drink?"

The sorcerer's eyes opened wide. He bent over and stared into Eli's face.

"What did you say?" he asked between clenched teeth.

Eli plunged ahead. "The three sisters were just a test, weren't they? You plan to curse the water in all of Israel." Jaktabar pivoted around to Saba.

"Did you hear him?" he asked. "He's not like you. He

does not need powers to know what will be. He has figured it out by himself. Such a mind would be helpful...

"I am glad you did not die with your parents. I am glad that I may still make use of you...teach you... Yes! That would be my greatest success, to command the child of Rabbi Ya'acov!"

"What are you talking about?" Eli exploded, suddenly realizing that Jaktabar had killed his parents.

"I am talking about power. About the ability to mold the future. One shot was all it took. And now you and your grandfather lie here before me, at my mercy. *As I planned!*"

Eli wanted to tell Jaktabar that what he said was not true. His parents died in an accident...on a dark road...in a fire. But he knew, even as he opened his mouth, that the sorcerer spoke the truth.

Suddenly there were shouts downstairs. Crash! Glass was breaking. Screams and shouts filled the hallway. A shot rang out. More cries. Jaktabar was already out the door and down the stairs. Eli started to follow, but Saba said, "No!"

The thunderous voice of the sorcerer carried through the house, and was followed by animal-like whelps. Then silence. A short sharp cry, like the one they had heard from Ahmed, pierced the air. Then the rat-ta-ta-tat of machine gun fire seemed everywhere. And, once again, silence.

Chapter 19

# Sins of the Servants

Close the door," Saba whispered to Eli. "Turn off the light and keep quiet." Eli did as he was told. It was pitch black in the room.

Then, something very strange occurred which Eli, even years later would have trouble believing ever really happened.

Rabbi Mordechai began to chant. Eli couldn't make out the words, except to note that he repeated the same words over and over again, his voice getting slightly higher with each repetition. A warm white light suddenly spread over Saba's face, faintly illuminating the room. Eli felt relaxed and soothed, even though deep down he was tense and very much afraid. Somehow, nothing seemed to really matter except Saba and his wonderful glow.

Eli thought he heard footsteps. The door flung open and three of Jaktabar's men rushed headlong into the room, their guns and rifles pointed at Saba. From the light in the hallway, Eli could see that Saba was swaying gently, his eyes closed, his voice a mere whisper.

The three Arabs stopped in their tracks, almost falling over one another in their desire not to go near Rabbi Mordechai. Eli was sure they would shoot his grandfather, from fear if for no other reason, but he was wrong. Gently, Rabbi Mordechai called to each of the three men by name.

As they stared at him, bewildered, Saba whispered to each in turn his life history. Where he was born, his parents' names, and, most tellingly, what sins he had committed since joining Jaktabar. The men began to shake and fell to their knees, openly crying. But this was not the end.

Rabbi Mordechai went on to explain what each man was supposed to accomplish in this world, and how he had failed in his mission. As he spoke, the men began wailing loudly, attesting to the fact that they somehow knew Rabbi Mordechai was speaking the truth.

"You Mahmud, were to have been a rich and prosperous businessman, honored and loved by many. But you chose to use your abilities to cheat others, to steal in the name of the Evil One.

"You, Rashid, have the heart of a poet. You can feel the pain and suffering of others and translate these emotions into words that could have brought you fame and honor. But instead you chose to cause pain and suffering to others, forcing your soul to suffer in silence.

"And you, Jabril, you have most betrayed your destiny, for you should have been a healer, a doctor, destined to save lives. Instead you torture and maim, creating dread and revulsion among your people."

The men, still kneeling before Saba, trembled and wept. They begged forgiveness and pleaded for him to say no more.

Then the old rabbi turned his head, opened his eyes and fixed his gaze on Eli.

Do not be afraid Eli, a voice inside his mind said. All things are possible with faith, and faith is the root of all things. I have much to show you, but little time left, so look Eli...look at your future.

A tear appeared in Saba's eye. Eli saw the tear shimmering in the unearthly glow that surrounded his grandfather's face, and in an instant he saw what his soul was to become. It was terrifying, and yet, guided by his grandfather's presence, he realized that what he was witnessing was just one of the roads he could take in his life. But, it was the future his Saba wanted for him.

In an instant it was gone. All that remained was the tear. And now the tear held new meaning, for it told Eli that his grandfather would not be part of his journey through life.

When Saba finally looked away, the light on his face flickered and faded out. He suddenly appeared shrunken and drained. He reached out his hands and the Arabs sprang forward to kiss them. Saba blessed them and then rose and walked towards the door. He put his hand on Eli's shoulder for support and then turned to the men.

"Promise me, before God, that you and your children after you will never harm this young man or his family. He is my son. Whatever is done to him is done to me. I will be watching."

The three men bowed low as they gave their solemn pledge. Then Saba, leaning heavily on his grandson, headed downstairs.

Chapter 20

# The Bloomes Arrive

Rabbi Mordechai told Eli to bring him the treasure box. In Jaktabar's study Eli found an opened parchment spread out on the desk. A dark oilskin bag was stuffed inside the box. He rolled up the document, closed the treasure box and left the study.

In the living room, the bodies of Jaktabar and the last guard assigned to them lay in a pool of blood. The sorcerer was riddled with bullet holes. It appeared to have taken the whole clip to bring him down. Wrapped around his neck were the coils of the hookah, its glass base smashed and the rancid water inside permeating the room with a putrid odor. Eli was shocked by the sight of the dead bodies, but Saba did not turn his head to look at them.

"Should I call Moshe?" Eli asked, as they stepped onto the front porch.

"I called him already," Saba said quietly.

This time Eli did not need to ask how he had done so.

They passed the box of bones which was in the front yard. Saba pointed to a gasoline can inside the van and Eli dragged it out and poured the gasoline into the box. Then Saba struck a match and threw it in.

The night sky was clear except for a plume of black smoke that spiralled from the box of bones. Eli heard the crackling of the bones as Saba and he turned down the dirt road toward the village. He felt proud, and a little sad, that Saba needed his help to walk. What was it that Moshe had said about the 36 righteous ones holding up the world? Saba certainly looked like he had done his share.

Headlights turned in from the highway, and they heard the familiar clatter of Moshe's taxi. Moshe jumped out and opened the passenger door, his pistol in his right hand.

"I never question the requests of Rabbi Mordechai," Moshe said to Eli, as he put the car in gear. "Even when he comes to me in a dream."

Back on the highway to Tzfat, Moshe blessed God and said, "As long as you are all right, Saba, I don't need to know anything else. How you got rid of the Evil One, I don't have to know. I have the merit to be your driver and if God wishes me to know, He will reveal it to me."

Saba nodded gently and smiled. "Then I don't need to tell you."

"Of course to hear from your own words is always the best."

"Later," Saba said with a faint smile to Eli.

"Eli, your parents called," Moshe said, changing the

*He felt proud, and a little sad, that Saba needed
his help to walk.*

subject. "They have arrived in Israel and are staying at the Rimon Inn here in Tzfat. I told them you and Saba went on a sightseeing trip and would be back tonight. You must decide what to tell them."

Eli was about to ask his grandfather, when Rabbi Mordechai volunteered. "The less the better."

Eli held the treasure box in his lap. He wanted to ask Saba if he could open it, but the old rabbi placed his hand on Eli's, and he knew he would still have to wait.

They first stopped at Rabbi Mordechai's house to wash up and change clothes. Eli was hungry but didn't want to keep his parents waiting.

When they pulled up to the hotel, Eli's parents ran out to greet him. Eli flew into their arms, and Saba shook hands with Mr. Bloome. Twelve years had passed since they had stood in a courtroom in Tzfat waiting for the judges to decide the fate of the young orphan.

"You have kept your promise," Saba said, gesturing towards Eli. "You have raised him according to the Torah and have prepared him for his destiny. May you be blessed in this world and the next."

Eli's mother blinked back tears and took Eli's hand. "Come, let's eat dinner," she said, leading the way into the hotel.

The Bloomes couldn't help but notice how almost everyone stood up as Rabbi Mordechai entered the dining room.

"You must tell me how you spent the day," Mrs. Bloome beamed, as they sat down. A basket of bread was put on the table and Eli jumped up to help Rabbi

Mordechai go and wash.

"He has certainly learned to honor his grandfather," Mr. Bloome commented.

"He and his Saba seem inseparable," Mrs. Bloome added, a tiny note of jealousy in her voice.

After Rabbi Mordechai and Eli returned and recited the blessing, the discussions began in earnest.

Suddenly Mrs. Bloome said, "Eli, you didn't bring your suitcase. I certainly hope you're planning on staying with us."

Eli nodded, busily swallowing a mouthful of food. "We just got into town and I wanted to come straight to see you," he said.

"It'll just take me 10 minutes to pack and then I'll be back. As a matter of fact," Eli added, gulping down the last of his soda, "maybe we should go back now before it gets really late."

Everyone agreed. The three men joined in the thanksgiving prayers said at the end of the meal and then everyone returned to Moshe who was dozing in his cab.

"You must really thank your grandfather for showing you around," Mrs. Bloome said. "I hope he hasn't been any trouble," she said to Rabbi Mordechai.

"He is a *m'chaya*, a pleasure to have around," Saba told her. "And a big help every time I needed him."

Rabbi Mordechai then thanked the Bloomes for the meal and gestured to Moshe that it was time to go.

On the drive back to Saba's house, the old rabbi told Eli, "We shall open the treasure tomorrow. Spend time with your parents now."

"But what if they ask me questions?"

"Silence is a fence for wisdom. Keep things simple and they will be happy."

When Eli returned to the hotel with his bags, his parents were waiting for him. They had rented a suite with two bedrooms. As soon as he settled in, they began asking questions about the flight, what he had been doing, what Saba was like, and whether he had been preparing for his Bar Mitzvah. Eli answered their questions with generalities, saying his visit to Israel was the most wonderful experience of his life. His parents could see he was tired so they soon told him to go to bed.

As he was turning in, Eli could hear his mother say to his father, "It's been a healing experience for him. See how quiet and relaxed he is?"

"I guess we didn't need to worry about terrorists," said Mr. Bloome. "Tzfat seems very peaceful, isolated from all that."

"Yes," sighed Mrs. Bloome, "Thank God."

## Chapter 21

# The Power of the Treasure

The next morning Eli was on his way out the door when his father entered the living room, wearing striped pajamas and slippers.

"Up so early?" Mr. Bloome said with a yawn. "Where are you going?"

"To Saba's, to pray," Eli answered, secretly thinking of the treasure.

His father perked up. "Can you wait for me? I'd love to come along."

Eli hesitated. He didn't want to hurt his father's feelings, but he certainly didn't want his father tagging along when he and Saba opened the treasure.

"Maybe you can meet us," Eli suggested, looking at his watch. "I'm really late, they have probably begun already."

"Oh come on son," his father coaxed, heading for his bedroom, "it will only take me a minute to get dressed."

His mother called from their bedroom, "Eli, wait for

your father, dear."

"I want to," he called back, "but Saba prays very early and I'm already late."

Mrs. Bloome came out of the bedroom, visibly upset. "I'm not a rabbi, but I think it's more important to pray with your father. I think even your grandfather would agree to that."

Eli knew his mother was right. The only way out of this dilemma was to tell the truth.

"You're right Mom, sorry," he said contritely. "The truth is, this is the morning Saba said he was going to give me my inheritance and I wanted, well, I thought it would be better with just the two of us."

"At 5:15 in the morning?" Mrs. Bloome asked, genuinely surprised. "Isn't it a bit early to read a will?"

"It's not early for Saba," Eli quickly replied, feeling he was gaining some ground. "He stays up all night learning. I'll try to be back soon. Honest."

"Let him go, Eileen," his father said, coming to his aid. "I could use a little extra sleep, and anyway, the two of us will be praying together for weeks to come."

Eli was touched by his father's words. He realized that his father was giving him a chance to say goodbye to Saba in his own way.

Eli smiled, said a quick "thanks" and left, closing the door with a sigh of relief.

Actually, Mr. and Mrs. Bloome were a bit relieved themselves. They didn't especially enjoy sharing Eli with his new-found "Saba." They felt that the quicker the inheritance was put out of the way, the sooner they would all be able to go on with their lives.

Eli found his grandfather in the old synagogue he had visited on the Sabbath. Rabbi Mordechai kept a prayerbook opened in front of him during the service, but he never opened his eyes. He gently swayed to his own soul's rhythm and continued praying, even after most of the other men had finished and gone home.

When they finally got back to Rabbi Mordechai's house, they sat down to some tea and biscuits and Saba took the metal box and the scroll and placed them on the table.

"Rabbi Ya'acov!" Saba cried, examining the contents of the box. "Very soon Rabbi Ya'acov, very soon we will be together."

Hearing his grandfather say these words made Eli very sad. Saba is the real treasure, he thought as he looked at the wrinkled wonderful face of his grandfather. What good is a box of gold if it means I won't have my grandfather?

Saba turned to him and smiled. "If I learned a thousand years, I would not know half of what my grandfather Rabbi Ya'acov knew. What he has left here is priceless."

He continued reading the scroll, then opened the box and took out the oilskin bag. Eli watched as Saba untied the string and pulled out a faded pair of tefillin. These were small black boxes which Eli, like other religious Jewish males, wore, from the age of 13. The tefillin straps were faded and brittle. Saba examined the tefillin as a jeweler would a priceless gem; his face shining as he turned the ancient boxes this way and that.

"More valuable than gold, more priceless than sil-ver..." he sang.

After a moment he looked over at his grandson. Eli couldn't really understand why his grandfather was mak-ing such a fuss over an old pair of tefillin.

"Disappointed? You do not know what a treasure this is! These tefillin were worn by Rabbi Ya'acov ben Orah himself. In his will he writes that anyone who wears these tefillin with pure intentions will be rewarded—" He paused, fixing Eli with a serious look. "Remember what you saw before we left Jaktabar's house? A bit of that power will be yours each time you wear these tefillin."

Eli gazed at Saba and then at the tefillin. That kind of power was beyond awesome. It was without a doubt the power of the prophets.

"Of course, it may be many years before you under-stand the value of your inheritance," said Saba, continu-ing to stare at Eli, "Or you may experience it very soon. It all depends on you."

Something occurred to Eli.

"Saba," he asked, "if Rabbi Ya'acov left only his te-fillin, why did Jaktabar want it so badly? He's not Jewish. What good is it to him?"

"He wanted this scroll," said Saba, pointing to the parchment. "You see, Rabbi Ya'acov was an expert in the Book of Creation. Jaktabar felt that his will might reveal the secrets of creating life. Jaktabar wanted these secrets for his own purposes. In many ways he was a genius in mysticism and magic. Who knows what he might have been able to do with these plans."

"Can we — I mean you — create life from these plans?" asked Eli.

"First let's worry about the plans for our own lives, before we try and create new ones!" laughed Saba.

Eli saw that his grandfather was in a good mood so he decided to ask the questions that had been bothering him ever since they had escaped Jaktabar.

"Saba," he said, "there is an awful lot I don't understand about what has happened to us these last few days. Especially about our escape from the sorcerer. I mean, how was it that Jaktabar's men didn't attack us when they came into the room? How did you know so much about each one? And what did that flower you crushed have to do with what happened?" Eli asked his questions almost in one breath, afraid he might not have a chance later.

"The followers of Islam, like us, believe in one God who is the master of all. They respect prayer and when Jaktabar's men came into our room, they immediately realized I was in contact with my inner soul; the soul that speaks to God. They could not — would not — harm us. It was an easy matter for me to tap into their own souls. That is my purpose in creation. Then, when I helped them tap into their own inner souls, they were incapable of harming us. They could only thank us for freeing them.

"As to the flower, everything in creation has a power behind it. That flower arouses jealousy and violence which is rooted in the animal power in us. When someone has these passions close to the surface of his being, the flower causes them to be expressed violently, usually with very destructive results. The evils inside Jaktabar and his men were brought out and turned against each other. This is the nature of evil. It is never satisfied. It must always feed on something; either the good or itself. But in the end, evil is always destroyed, like the shell which holds the seed which ultimately becomes a flower."

## Chapter 22
# Saba's Birthday

After breakfast they went for a walk. Eli followed Saba through the ancient cemetery to the grave of Rabbi Ya'acov ben Orah. The old man circled the grave seven times, saying the psalms of King David and adding his own prayers. When he had finished, he asked forgiveness for his sins and said a special prayer for the dead. Pointing to an empty plot, a few feet down the slope from Rabbi Ya'acov's grave, Rabbi Mordechai said, "That will be my place."

It was difficult for Eli to accept what his grandfather had said. They had just gotten to know each other.

Saba put a hand on Eli's shoulder. "Remember," he said, "under the ground, the roots have no sunlight. And above ground, the leaves have no water. For the Tree of Life to grow and spread its branches, it depends on the roots and the leaves working together." He paused and added softly, "I am the roots, and you are the leaves. Working together we are the ultimate expression of the

Tree of Life."

Eli nodded.

"In two days," Saba said, "it will be my birthday. I will be 90 years old. That will be my last day. But leaving this old, tired body, doesn't mean I'm leaving you. I will be free to return to the Kingdom of Light, to live in harmony and eternal peace. But I will always, always have an ear open to hear you."

Eli bit his lip and tears trickled down his face.

"We shall be together always," Saba said, trying to soothe him.

"It won't be the same," Eli said with difficulty.

"No, it won't be," Saba said. "You'll have to listen more closely to hear my voice. It will be like a distant echo in your heart, like the wind carrying a message from heaven. But I will help you. Never fear."

The next day Saba went through his papers. Instead of being sullen and depressed, Saba sang his morning prayers with great zest and hummed to himself. Anyone looking at him would think he was preparing for a vacation. Seeing how sad Eli had become, he turned to his grandson and said, "If only you could see where I am going, you would not be sad. You would be happy for me. Come now, bring me my flute."

Eli brought the old wooden instrument and Saba began playing a cheerful tune. The notes fluttered like a butterfly in full flight. Saba stood up and danced a few steps, inviting Eli to join him. But Eli found this too painful. He felt many emotions running through him, but joy was not one of them. Yet Saba urged him on.

"Dance!" he cried, "Tomorrow is my birthday. It is a simcha!"

With a heavy heart, Eli forced himself to dance with his Saba. He understood that in some ways, Rabbi Mordechai had already left this world.

I'm not sure he was ever fully a part of this world to begin with, he thought to himself.

## Chapter 23
# Swirling Souls

Eli spent the next day with his parents. He tried to show them around town, but he was tense and irritable.

"What's the matter, Eli?" his father asked, concerned. "We promised we wouldn't leave until the end of the week. You'll have plenty of time to say goodbye to your grandfather."

"No I won't," Eli answered solemnly. "Tomorrow's his birthday."

"Terrific," his mother exclaimed. "What shall we buy him?"

"Tomorrow is also the day he says he will die," Eli explained.

"What?" both of his parents exclaimed at the same time.

"It's a long story, and I'm not even sure I understand it. But somehow, many of the great rabbis die on the day they were born. It's some kind of tradition going back to

Moses. It's like they've completed a circle or something."

His parents were silent. Then his father said, "Then perhaps you should be spending this last day with your grandfather, son."

Eli looked up at his father, and then at his mother, and fell into their arms, thanking them for being so understanding.

They returned to the hotel where Eli got some things, and kissing his parents goodbye, headed back to Rabbi Mordechai's house.

When he entered the house, he put his clothes away and pulled up a chair next to his Saba who was studying in his sing-song voice. Without stopping his tune, Saba lifted his hand and put it on Eli's head, gently stroking him. Eli opened up a book and began to read, echoing the rhythm of his grandfather's tune.

They stayed like that for many hours, grandfather and grandson, until at last it was time to go to bed.

On that final day, Eli rose early and found his grandfather sitting in the kitchen stirring a glass of dark tea.

"You see this," Saba said as though he had been waiting for him, "you see the tea leaves? They're at the bottom of the glass. The spoon stirs them and what happens? All the leaves rise to the surface, swirling in a spiral. Then, take the spoon out and the leaves continue turning as if on their own. Around and around they go, each leaf dancing its own dance, slowly sinking to the bottom where they finally come to rest again."

Eli gazed at the cup. He had no idea what Saba was talking about.

"Explain this to me," Saba asked him.

Eli glanced at his grandfather and shrugged.

"Remember the leaves in the cemetery," Saba suggested, turning the spoon in the glass.

Eli tried to remember.

"Concentrate," said Saba.

After several moments, Saba prompted, "The leaves are souls and the spoon is the hand of God, stirring the souls to life."

"I understand," Eli suddenly exclaimed. "When the spoon is removed the leaves keep swirling. It looks as if God has gone away, but He's only hidden. When the leaves sink to the bottom, they are returning to heaven. Then God stirs them up again."

Saba shouted joyously and blessed Eli seven times.

No one knew how the news that Saba had foretold the day of his passing spread throughout Tzfat. The fact that Rabbi Mordechai was going to die on his birthday was of special importance. Only the most righteous merited to die, like Moses, on the anniversary of their birth.

People came to pay their respects and ask for blessings; among them many of the sages Eli had seen on Sabbath night. They entered Saba's room with awe on their faces. The old rabbi received them with kindness until early in the morning.

Moshe went down the line of visitors, reminding them that there was not much time; they should speak briefly and to the point.

The three sisters came. The oldest sister cried bitterly. saying, "I wanted the Rabbi to perform the marriage

*"...you see the tea leaves? They're at the bottom of the glass.
The spoon stirs them and what happens?"*

ceremony under the canopy, the *chupa*, at our wedding."

Saba comforted her and gave her a special blessing that she might bear many children.

Eli's parents were the last to leave Saba. They thanked him for the opportunity of raising his grandson. They promised to continue guiding him in the way of the Torah. Then, they went back to their hotel to wait for Eli.

Eli, for his part, would not leave Saba's side. He wanted — needed — to be there when his grandfather finally left this world.

When all the guests had gone, Saba got up from the couch and went to stand by the window. Eli came to his side.

Rabbi Mordechai said, "Remember, the tefillin are yours and must be given only to your children and their children. Together we will build strong lasting branches. This is Rabbi Ya'acov's wish, and part of his inheritance.

"Now let me bless you." Saba placed both hands upon Eli's head. "May God bless you with the gift of true vision. May He help you discover the path that is your soul's destiny. Learn from your teachers and become a teacher after them. Devote yourself always to the future of our people, for they are your future, your past and your present, and from them will come the Redeemer, the Messiah. Know too that there are those who have been selected by the Maker of Souls, Blessed be He, to watch over our people, to fight the legions of Darkness, and protect the Light that was formed at Creation. I pray that you are one of these people as was your great-grandfather, and his father before him." Then pressing hard on Eli's head, Saba almost shouted, "May it be God's will!"

Rabbi Mordechai bent over and kissed his head. Then he whispered, "You will know when you hear the wind." He quietly laid down on his bed.

Eli felt chills go up and down his spine. He couldn't move. He was afraid that if he moved the power of the blessing would be broken. And yet he didn't really understand all his grandfather had said. What Light? What destiny?

And then, as if a veil had been lifted from his mind, he suddenly understood. The 36 righteous ones! The pillars of the world. Their legacy was his inheritance. He was being blessed and also initiated into the ranks of his great-grandfather, and Eli knew how little he understood, and yet how important that little was.

He thought of the Kingdom of Light where Saba was going and realized that this must be part of the Light that God created on the first day of Creation and then hid, lest the powers of Darkness use the Light for their own purposes. This Light had been given over for safekeeping to the 36 upon whose shoulders the world now stood. That was why a man like Saba could know things he had not been witness to, or what would happen in the future. His feet might be rooted here on earth, but his heart and mind were in heaven, in touch with the Kingdom of Light. For the first time Eli understood why his grandfather and those like him were called kabbalists: those who receive the hidden Light!

Eli realized he too was part of that Tree. In fact, every

human being was connected by the branches of Light. Even those who do evil. And that was why Saba wanted to see if Jaktabar would come back, abandon his former ways, just like the evil son in the story.

It was too much for Eli. His mind was racing from idea to idea like a pinball. The responsibility felt too heavy, too awesome. He wanted to be just another Bar Mitzvah boy. But most of all, he wanted to cry.

When he turned to face his grandfather, he saw that Saba's eyes were closed. His hands were neatly folded in front of him. His feet were facing the door. His beard had never looked so white and his lips were pursed, as if in a kiss.

Moshe came in and began to moan bitterly.

"See how he lies there," he cried, "so like Moses our Teacher, who was kissed by God and whose body remains forever pure and whole. God has kissed him. God has kissed our revered Rabbi Mordechai and taken back His soul..."

Chapter 24

# The Kingdom of Light

Saba's body, wrapped in his prayer shawl, was placed in the ground near the grave of Rabbi Ya'acov ben Orah. A large myrtle stood there, and as the wind blew across from Mount Meron, a few leaves spiralled to the ground. Leaning against the tree, watching the leaves, Eli felt Saba still at his side.

The following day, Eli and his parents left Tzfat for a rented apartment in the Old City of Jerusalem. Eli knew he had to prepare for his Bar Mitzvah now, but his mind was filled with thoughts of Saba. Only when learning with Rabbi Weiss, his Bar Mitzvah tutor, did the loneliness pass.

Rabbi Steven Weiss was a middle-aged American rabbi who had come to live in Israel, soon after his third, and last child, made aliyah. He worked as a high school English teacher, but gave Bar Mitzvah lessons to many of the American children who felt more comfortable taking lessons from someone they could relate to from the "old country." Eli studied his Bar Mitzvah reading, the portion called Korach as well as Talmud and Prophets several hours each evening.

Eli knew his Torah reading almost by heart, but he was nervous about leading the services. He didn't understand all the words in the prayer book and he was afraid that when he had to recite out loud, he would lose track of what he was saying and make a mistake.

One evening Rabbi Weiss asked to see Eli's tefillin. "I want to make sure they are kosher," he explained.

"But my grandfather gave them to me," said Eli.

"If they're old," said the rabbi gently, "there's a good chance the parchments inside are cracked or faded. They must be checked."

The next morning Eli brought the little oilskin bag containing the ancient tefillin.

"These belonged to Rabbi Ya'acov ben Orah," said Eli. "He was my great-great grandfather, and he lived in Tzfat. Have you ever heard of him?"

"There are many great rabbis that I've never heard of," Rabbi Weiss said. "Who gave them to you?"

"My Saba, Rabbi Mordechai."

"And how did he get them?"

Eli did not know where to begin. The three sisters? The house of mourning? The curse of Jaktabar?

"Never mind," said the rabbi. "I know the best sofer, tefillin scribe, in Jerusalem. He will look at your tefillin and tell us if they are kosher."

That night Eli told his parents what Rabbi Weiss had said.

"We can always get you a new pair of tefillin, if there's any problem," said his mother.

"No," said Eli, "I want to wear these. Only these."

"Well," said his father. "We'll wait and see what the sofer says."

The next morning Eli went with Rabbi Weiss to Mea Shearim, the Hassidic section of Jerusalem. Here, almost everyone dressed in the black hats and long black coats that were the trademark of the Jews in Europe before World War II.

As they made their way through the crowded streets, Eli held the tefillin tightly.

In a narrow alley off Mea Shearim street, they entered a little doorway beneath a tarnished copper sign. The shop smelled of ink, dust and leather. Several old pairs of tefillin were on display in the dusty window-box. Behind the counter sat an old man with a white beard peering through a magnifying glass. He was studying a small parchment by the light of a naked bulb dangling from the ceiling. He did not notice the visitors. Picking up a razor, he sliced through the seams of a tefillin box with the precision of a surgeon. The blade pierced Eli's heart. Would he cut open Rabbi Ya'acov's tefillin like that? And what would he decide? Could the treasure he had risked his life for be suddenly declared "unfit for use?"

The sofer then took out the parchment from the box and examined it, running his fingers along each letter of each word. Rabbi Weiss shuffled his feet and the old scribe looked up. He gingerly folded up the parchment and put it aside.

Then the sofer greeted Rabbi Weiss warmly in Yiddish. Eli did not understand what they were saying. He whispered to his tutor and the rabbi switched smoothly into Hebrew. Rabbi Weiss asked Eli for the tefillin and Eli reluctantly handed over the oilskin bag. To his surprise, the scribe spoke to him in English.

"Who did these belong to?"

"A rabbi from Tzfat named Rabbi Ya'acov ben Orah—"

The scribe's eyes opened wide. He became very animated. "The author of *The Kingdom of Light*?" he asked, as though not able to believe his ears. "Rabbi Weiss," the scribe said, anxious to share his knowledge, "do you know whose tefillin these are? One of the greatest *gedolim* of the last century! His commentaries on the Etz Haim (Tree of Life) are studied to this day. He was an *illuy*, a genius."

The scribe's hands began shaking. He asked Eli how he had obtained them. When Eli said he was a descendant of Rabbi Ya'acov, the sofer took off his glasses, got up from his table and came over to look at him closely. He shook his hand and cried, "*Gevalt!*"

Returning to his table, he examined the tiny boxes like a jeweler eyeing a priceless stone. Then he took up his knife.

"No," yelled Eli, unable to contain himself. "Don't!"

"How else can I see what's inside?" said the scribe, holding the tefillin to the light. "Don't worry. This is a great honor for me, to check the tefillin of Rabbi Ya'acov ben Orah. I will be careful."

The scribe cut the seams open and pried the parchments out of their tiny compartments. With great care, he unbound the tiny scrolls and lay them flat on a felt pad. As he examined the lettering he sighed and praised God in Hebrew several times.

While the examination was going on, the door opened and a man in a stylish English suit entered. The scribe glanced up and then quickly rose from his table to greet the customer. They also spoke in English and Eli understood that the gentleman was a collector of Judaica from London. He had come to Israel to expand his collection.

"You have come on the right day," said the scribe. "This young man has brought in the most marvelous tefillin I have ever seen. They are undoubtedly the work of a master of the late 18th-century Sefardi school. *Mekubalim Gedolim!* Great Kabbalists. I have seen this hand before, in the tefillin of the Abuchatzera and Alefandri families, but never so well preserved."

"How much do you think they are worth?" asked the man in a precise British accent.

"I would say," said the scribe as he turned the parchment over in his hands, "based on what I have heard others from the same period have been sold for...hmm..." The scribe peered intently at the writing. "The condition — miraculous — they are perfect. Not one crack. They must have been stored in a cool damp place. Hmm... I would say — " he glanced at Eli, "not less than $18,000."

Rabbi Weiss whistled. "Well," he said, "sounds like you really did inherit a treasure."

Eli's mouth went dry. The shop seemed to close in on him. Eighteen thousand dollars for Rabbi Ya'acov's tefillin? The number floated through his mind. The collector seemed mesmerized by the tefillin.

"If you say they are worth $18,000 Rabbi Yiddel, then I accept that. And I offer it to you, young man," he said, smiling at Eli.

"I don't want to sell," Eli whispered.

The scribe slipped off his glasses and gave the boy a look.

"You don't want to sell?"

"No," said Eli, louder and more emphatically. "I don't want the money. I want the tefillin — sewn up — please."

The scribe looked at Rabbi Weiss.

"Eli, perhaps you would like to talk it over with your parents? Eighteen thousand dollars is — "

"I don't want to sell Rabbi Ya'acov's tefillin!" Eli insisted. His face flushed red, his ears burned. Tears brimmed over his eyes. No one could make him sell his birthright. No one.

"A little tzaddik," said the scribe. "Very well, Mr. Breakstone, today was not your day. But who knows? We have other things — just let me take care of this young man."

After the scribe sewed up the tefillin, Eli and Rabbi Weiss left the shop. The oilskin bag felt good in Eli's hands.

The next morning he returned to his studies. But no matter how hard he tried, he couldn't concentrate. He felt as though he was missing something, as though he had lost something more valuable than even his tefillin.

Saba. It wasn't the same without him.

How could he celebrate becoming a Jewish man without his grandfather there? Saba was the one who had made him into a man. He had taught him to think with his soul, and opened his eyes to the mysteries of life.

After learning with Rabbi Weiss that evening, Eli decided to spend some time in the Old City before going home. The Western Wall drew him like a magnet, and he headed down the wide stone staircase towards the site of the ancient Temple. The main plaza was busy. Looking for a quieter spot, Eli entered the large hall to the left of the Wall. He found a quiet corner near one of the many wooden arks where Torah scrolls were kept. He picked up a prayer book, pulled up a chair, and opened to a page of Psalms. He wanted to give thanks to God for everything; for his parents, his grandfather, the miracles and mystical experiences he had been through. But in the end, he laid his head down on the prayer book and cried.

He heard himself sobbing, as if he were far removed from his body, and he felt free and clean and whole. Is this what the soul feels at death, he thought, as a wave of sleep finally overtook him.

Chapter 25

# To Hear the Wind

Eli was awakened by a tap on the shoulder. An old man in a long black coat stood before him.

"You are Eliyahu?" he said in broken English. "The grandson of Rabbi Mordechai?"

Eli was too startled to reply.

"You are, yes? I see Yankees. That is the name of your hat?"

Eli absently touched his cap. "I don't understand. Who are you?"

"We learned together one night."

Eli strained to recognize the man, but couldn't.

"Shabbos in Tzfas," the old man said. "Abuhav Beis Knesses. Your grandfather is our teacher."

Eli nodded, recalling that wonderful night.

"You remember now," the old man said with a soothing voice.

"Saba is dead," Eli whispered.

"His body, but not his soul. Here is my number." The

man handed him a card. "Your grandfather was a tzad-dik. He commanded us to show you. So do not fear, we are here for you."

"Show me? Show me what?" Eli asked, more con-fused than ever. He stood up and realized that he was inches taller than the old man. It made him uncomfort-able.

"Your grandfather has taken care of all this. You will know Eliyahu, grandson of Rabbi Mordechai. You will know when you hear the wind."

Having finished what he came to say, the old man turned and melted into the gathering crowd. Eli looked at the card. There was only a telephone number. No name or address. Just black numbers on a white card.

But what did the old man mean about hearing the wind? Weren't those the same cryptic words Saba had uttered before his death?

As he headed home, Eli felt certain that Saba had known how he would feel, and had sent his strange col-league to Jerusalem to comfort him.

But how had the old rabbi known where to find him?

## Chapter 26

# Attack in the Jewish Quarter

Before first light, Eli took his oilskin bag and went with his father toward the Old City. Even as dawn rose, the stars stood above the Tower of David like silent sentries around the castle of a king.

Eli and his father entered through the Jaffa Gate. Zigzagging through the cobbled streets, they came to a spot where the alley split in two directions. Eli thought they should go right, but his father insisted they go left, so they went left. The street wound around a house, dipped down under an arch, then rose steeply into a narrow alleyway.

"Dad, are you sure you know where we're going?" Eli asked.

"Well, I thought I did," his father answered, sounding anything but sure. "I think if we keep heading this way..." Mr. Bloome said, trying to get his bearings.

They continued down the corridor through a low arch. Step by step, Eli began noticing a distinct difference in the look of the houses.

"Uh, Dad," he said, tugging at his father's jacket, "we're not in the Jewish quarter anymore. This looks like the Moslem quarter."

Eli's father stood on the dark empty street, before a line of closed shops covered with steel doors. The air was heavy with spices and the smell of burning oil.

"I can't believe it," his father said, angry with himself. "I should have listened to you. Instead, now we're lost in the Moslem quarter on the morning of your Bar Mitzvah. That's perfect. I'm glad your mother's not here. Let's try and double back," he suggested. "Maybe we'll get lucky and find a policeman or a soldier."

They did an about-face. Down the street they heard the plaintive cry of a cat, then a warning hiss from another cat. Their animal voices had an eerie human quality.

"This is not where I want to be," said Mr. Bloome.

Eli did not answer. He thought, What would Saba do? Saba, he realized, would never have gotten lost like this. So, he whispered a few words, asking God to guide them safely out of trouble.

"There's a light down there," his father said, pointing to the entranceway to a shop just below street level.

They approached the shop, climbed down some steps and knocked on the door. No answer. Eli gently tried the door. It opened easily and he poked his head through the doorway. Then a burst of flame seem to reach out for Eli as his father pulled him back, just in time.

"Easy Eli," Mr. Bloome comforted him. "I think it's

just a bakery. They're firing up the ovens."

A light went on in a window above them. Muffled voices hurled curses at them in Arabic.

"Great," Mr. Bloome said, "now we've woken the entire neighborhood." He pulled his son's arm. "Let's get out of here," he commanded. They both started to run.

"Wait," Eli said, "wait."

They stopped, their breath coming fast and loud. Eli felt fear creeping like a spider in his heart. He banished the fear with a mighty effort.

"We've got to think clearly," he told his father.

Mr. Bloome watched his son, waiting for him to speak.

"First, we know the Kotel is to the East," Eli said. "And the sun rises in the east." He pointed to the first rays of the sun as they appeared over the Arab shops. "That means, the Jewish quarter is...that way!"

"Okay," Mr. Bloome agreed, wondering how his son knew this. "I'll follow you."

Just then they heard a rumble of footsteps up the street, and a rhythmic shout like the chant of an angry mob. The frightful noise steadily approached them. Eli took his father's arm and pulled him into a dark doorway. Down the alley, at a distance of about 100 feet, a gang of young men turned a corner. Eli and his father watched in terror as the mob came closer. The shadows were now their only protection. Five or six men, their heads and faces covered in kafiyas, were wielding torches, knives, steel pipes and clubs. They were banging on doors. Their chant grew louder. Eli could barely distinguish the words,

"Palestine! Palestine!"

Eli, his heart pounding wildly, suddenly remembered the scene from his dreams of the massacre in Tzfat. It was happening again! His grip was like a vice on his father's arm.

"Dad, we've got to do something!" Eli whispered.

"Where are the police?" his father's frightened voice asked.

"I don't know! Let's wait till they pass."

The mob was almost upon them. Crazed black eyes peered out behind cloth scarves. Torches poured swirling smoke into the air.

It had all happened before, Eli thought. The nightmare was coming true before his very eyes!

Miraculously, the gang passed without seeing them. Eli and his father poked their heads out and watched as the men went up the street and turned into another alley. Eli, leading his father, crept quietly into the street and started after them. His father was not far behind.

Suddenly, Eli heard a cry. His father had tripped and fallen. He was holding his ankle.

"Dad!" he whispered, returning to his father.

Mr. Bloome, obviously in pain, pulled himself up to a sitting position. "I think it's only sprained," he said. "You better go ahead. If you pass a phone, call the police! I'll be right behind you."

A light went on in the window above them. They both looked up.

"Go on," said Mr. Bloome, slowly rising. "I'll catch up."

Eli reluctantly left his father and ran up the street to the alley where the gang had turned. He smelled the burning kerosine of their torches, and soon saw the flames leaping up into the sky. He kept at least 50 feet behind them, staying in the shadows beneath the awnings of the shops, running swiftly, then stopping to cover, then taking off again. When the gang turned once more, their voices suddenly quieted, the torches were extinguished and they disappeared like ghosts at dawn.

Instantly, Eli recognized where he was. He had walked this street many times before. This was Rechov HaYehudim, the Street of the Jews, the entranceway to the Jewish Quarter.

Eli also realized that the major synagogue in this area was the famous Ramban Synagogue, only a few short streets ahead. He was certain that the gang was heading in that direction. He was undecided whether to follow his hunch or run to the police station. Then he realized that to get to the police station he would have to pass the synagogue anyway. He ran all out, hoping he would reach the synagogue before the mob.

Suddenly, like a pack of wolves converging on a kill, the gang emerged at the back entrance to the synagogue. A heavy axe flashed in the dim light from the Cardo, a sharp "Crash!" and the gang streamed into the synagogue. Eli was intent on running past the synagogue toward the police station when he hit upon an idea. Just beyond the building, several cars were parked. He reached the cars and began hitting their windows and fenders with his hands and feet. In a matter of seconds,

*Miraculously, the gang passed without seeing them.*

the ear-splitting cry of a dozen car alarms filled the Jewish Quarter. People came running from all directions, some in their bathrobes, some half-dressed, guns held high. The police were at the front of the synagogue in seconds. Meanwhile, spotting a vendor's cart, he sent it sailing into the back door of the synagogue. It was wedged tightly. Running swiftly, Eli took cover behind a palm tree.

As the police came charging through the front door, the Arabs came flying out back like frightened bats flying out of a cave. But they couldn't "fly" high enough to avoid the cart. Crash! Wham! They fell over one another shouting and screaming to get out. The gang was still trying to sort themselves out when they found a dozen automatic rifles aimed at them.

Eli remained hidden behind the palm tree, exhausted and shaking. A few moments later, his father came limping along. A policeman stopped him and told him to go home.

"You don't understand," Mr. Bloome explained, "My son is in there somewhere!"

"With them?" the policeman pointed at the youths lying on their stomachs with their hands cuffed behind their backs.

"No! He's American. I'm sure he must have sounded the alarm!"

Eli was about to call to his father, but thought better of it. The last thing he needed now — on his Bar Mitzvah day — was to spend hours being questioned by the police. The sun was up, and he wanted to get to the

Western Wall.

So, he dashed out of his hiding place and circled to the front of the synagogue.

"Dad," he yelled, "over here."

Mr. Bloome turned toward the sound of his voice. Eli raced over to his father. Holding out his arms, Mr. Bloome gave his son a hug. "How did you get over here? Did you call the police?" he asked.

"How's your leg?" Eli asked in return, purposely changing the subject.

"I think it's all right," Mr. Bloome said. "I was very lucky. Some old Arab man came out of his house and actually tore off his undershirt and tied the ankle. He wanted to call a doctor for me. He insisted I come inside his house for coffee," Mr. Bloome laughed, "but I told him, I'm a little busy at the moment."

Eli's father hugged him again, and laughing, they went off down the alley toward the Western Wall.

Chapter 27

# A Strange Bar Mitzvah Celebration

At the Western Wall or *Kotel*, as Israelis call it, people were arriving for the morning prayer. Eli and his father, realizing they still had more than an hour before the service was to start, decided to see some of the artifacts discovered beneath the Wall. They entered the underground hall and saw that a large metal door at the end was open. A tray of memorial candles filled the air with the scent of beeswax. The Rabbi of the Kotel, draped in a white prayer shawl, was just arriving. They followed him into a narrow tunnel, its stones damp and cold. The ceiling hung low over their heads.

Eli remembered hearing about similar tunnels leading to the center of the Temple Mount. A group of Kabbalists prayed in a small synagogue opposite the Temple Mount, only a stone's throw from the site said to have been the majestic Holy of Holies. The Ark of the Covenant which Moses had built 3,300 years ago to hold the Ten Commandments was thought to be buried beneath the Holy of Holies. All prophecy was said to emanate from this place.

Eli recalled reading that in an ironic twist, ever since the capture of this site by the Jews in 1967, the Israeli government forbade any Jew from entering the Temple Mount to pray. Only Moslems were permitted to worship on this holy site.

Eli followed behind the rabbi, but his father, while no longer limping, trailed further back. The tunnel seemed to go on and on. The Rabbi walked quickly; and Eli saw it was hard for his father to keep up. Finally, Eli stopped to wait for his father. When his father reached him they continued down the path, but the tunnel was empty.

They looked down the corridor as far as they could see. There was no sign of anyone. They continued walking until they came to a sign which said they were opposite the Holy of Holies. What seemed like an electric current flowed through Eli. He tried to shake it off, but it persisted.

"Are we lost again?" his father asked.

"No," Eli answered. The tingling became more intense. He closed his eyes for a moment and then, out of nowhere, he heard the wind blowing through the tunnel.

*"You will know when you hear the wind,"* came racing through his mind. Know what?

He listened for a long time.

"Eli," he heard his father call him, "Eli!" he said more frantically.

Eli opened his eyes.

"It's getting late. Maybe we should get back," his father suggested, looking at him strangely.

"What's the matter, Dad?" Eli asked.

"I don't know son, but your face, it took on this strange glow, like you had a temperature or something. Are you all right?"

Eli sighed. "I'm okay, Dad," he said, and wondering whether his father had just experienced what he had experienced, he asked, "You didn't hear the wind just now did you?"

"Wind, down here, what wind?"

"Nothing. Must have been an echo or something."

Before his father could say anything else, Eli led the way back.

They came to the steel gate and walked into the plaza of the Western Wall. Though it was still early, people were already streaming onto the plaza. There were businessmen catching a *minyan*, a service, before work, as well as scholars who sang their prayers with mystic fervor.

Eli heard a multitude of languages all around him as fathers and sons from all over the world came to Jerusalem to renew their connection to each other and their tradition. Women's cries mingled with the prayers of the men. Moroccans in striped robes and Yemenites with white turbans, Chassidim in long black coats and knickers, Russians and Ethiopians, Jews from Persia, Khurdistan and India — each group sang and danced as they had learned from their fathers and grandfathers. People threw nuts and candies at Bar Mitzvah boys reading from the Torah for the first time.

Eli chose a reading table close to the women's section where his mother and Mrs. Weiss were waiting. When it was time for his Bar Mitzvah service to begin, he took Rabbi Ya'acov's tefillin out of the oilskin bag. He had left his own tefillin, the ones he used since he turned 13, back in the apartment. Trembling, he unwrapped the straps from the boxes. He placed them on his head and arm and said the blessings.

He closed his eyes and, once again, he heard the wind. Only this time it seemed to emanate from within him. He felt the presence of...of the Sabbath. Worries, doubts and fears disappeared. He did not want to move or to speak. It was enough just to be there, with the wind, with the Sabbath.

He opened his eyes. It wasn't the Sabbath. It was Thursday, he reminded himself. Funny, how he felt the warm feeling he had felt at Saba's Sabbath table.

He began to recite the service out loud. Men from the immediate vicinity came to join in the service, offering their voices and prayers, as his "congregation" swelled from 10 to 20 to suddenly, almost 50 men.

His voice rose as he watched the words form images before his eyes.

*"Blessed is He who said, and it was!"* revealed to Eli the instant of creation, as light and dark swirled before his eyes.

*"Happy is the man who dwells in his house..."* and he saw his parents (could it be his parents?) laughing and

talking in their home, a little baby cuddled in his mother's arms.

*"Hear O Israel, the Lord our God the Lord is One!"* unfolded before him, as martyred Jews sang out this litany with their dying breaths. For a moment, Eli saw Rabbi Ya'acov and Jaktabar's great-grandfather peering into each other's eyes; the image smashed by the axe that fell unerringly toward Rabbi Ya'acov.

It went on and on.

People started to crowd around, sensing that something strange and wonderful was happening.

"Who is he?" someone asked.

"He seems possessed!" another exclaimed.

From all around men converged upon Eli's table. Each person felt a ray of light from the glowing face of the young boy penetrate his heart. Unable to control the outpouring of their souls, they too began to sing and pray out loud with all their strength.

Then Eli began to sway. And move. And dance. The people opened a circle for him as he twirled around and around. He held out his hands and as first one, then another person joined him, they were swept up in his rhythm, in his speed, in his light. Then the crowd, perhaps 100 people, joined in not just dancing but — as some would swear later on — flying with this young man whose face glowed with the warmth of the sun.

Eli felt the wind. It was cooling and soothing. He looked up and saw his grandfather playing his flute, dancing and crying, all at the same time.

"We are all one," Rabbi Mordechai whispered. "All

*The people opened a circle for him as he twirled
around and around.*

one with the Tree of Life."

Then Saba came and took his grandson's hand and helped Eli tame the wind, calm it, and send it flowing through his soul. "But remember, the wind, the spirit, is always to give to others," his grandfather told him, pointing to the people around him. "You must use it for them, for their happiness. Only then will it truly be yours."

Eli understood. He would be one of the branches that would reach out to give life to others.

Chapter 28

# The Old Rabbi Responds

Eli was sitting by the telephone. His parents watched him from the archway to the kitchen of their apartment in the Old City. Five days had passed since his Bar Mitzvah and they were worried. Since the experience at the Western Wall, he had not been the same young man. Most of the day he spent sitting in his room in silence, staring out the window. He ate little. When he wasn't praying or glancing at a book, he would pace like a prisoner awaiting the day of his release.

The only activity he did with his usual zest for life was to call on the telephone. Yet even this he did in a strange manner.

"He just dials, then waits and lets the phone ring and ring and ring," Mrs. Bloome said to her husband.

Mr. Bloome sighed. He understood that after the Bar Mitzvah there might be a little let down. But Eli seemed to have risen much higher and fallen much further than was normal. He did what he had to do, helping his mother in the apartment, walking with his father to the store or synagogue, running an errand when he was called on. But it was as if part of him wasn't there. Part of him was *still* at the Western Wall, dancing in the crowd, flying with the visions he had seen. People in the Old City who had witnessed the event greeted him as though he were something of a celebrity, yet he did not feel different than anyone else. His main concern was getting through to the telephone number written on the little white card. He wanted to speak to the mysterious rabbi, who had learned with Saba and knew him well. He felt he could trust him and would understand what he had gone through. Also, by contacting the man, he hoped to feel some of the closeness to his grandfather that he had felt before the Bar Mitzvah.

But no one ever answered the number. At first he was patient. Perhaps the man had left Jerusalem for a few days, perhaps he kept odd hours. But as the days wore on and there was still no answer, his patience wore thin and he became frustrated.

"Eli," his mother said, standing beside him as he dialed the number for perhaps the hundredth time. "Maybe it's not meant to be right now. Maybe you have to go on with your life without connecting with this man, and then later, who knows, if not this trip, then during another one, you'll meet him again."

Eli sighed. He fought off the pain in his heart that always seemed to be lurking there, trying to make him cry.

"I want to talk to him before we leave. It's important,

Mom. Really important."

Mr. Bloome knelt beside him. "Son, it is important. No one is denying that. It's just that we see how hard these past few days have been for you since your Bar Mitzvah and we want to help."

"Thank you, but there's nothing anyone can do. I want to talk to him. He knew Saba, and he would understand what happened at the Kotel. No one else seems to understand." He bit his lower lip, a mist in his eyes.

"What do you feel we don't understand?" his mother asked, trying not to sound too hurt.

Eli shook his head. "I can't put it into words. It's like... like Saba spoke to me from the other world. I saw him. He was there. We were together again."

"Well," said his father, "that's a wonderful thing. You know how many people have had such an experience? Maybe one in a million. You should feel lucky and thankful and happy to have had such a special connection to your grandfather, in so short a time."

"I do feel all those things," Eli said softly, in an unconvincing voice. "I just don't know what to do. I need to talk to the man who gave me this card."

The next day, Mr. Bloome came home and said, "Our flight is tonight, 12 Midnight. They had three cancellations and were able to take us." He motioned to his wife. They had already discussed it with Rabbi Weiss. It had been decided that the best thing for Eli would be to get him back to the States as soon as possible, to return to a normal life.

Almost on impulse, Eli went to the phone and dialed

the number again.

There was still the same insistent brrr...brrr...brrr at the other end of the line. He let it ring 20 times and hung up, dejected.

That night Eli and his father went to the Western Wall to pray the evening prayers for the last time. While his father joined a minyan, Eli went up and down the long high wall, staring at every person who looked like the little old rabbi who had given him the card. They all seemed to fit the description, and yet no one was an exact match. Finally, he gave up and went to pray. He sat by himself as he had before, beside an Ark of the Torah, his face only a few inches from the holy ancient stones. He could not concentrate enough to pray with a group, so he merely prayed with his own words, thanking God for all the good things He had given him, and then asking for one last meeting with the old rabbi before leaving Israel. During the prayer he wept and after he had dried his eyes, he felt a hand on his shoulder. He turned, thinking it was his father, but to his amazement, it was the old man.

"It's you!" he cried with joy. "I've been calling you day and night for almost a week! Where have you been?"

The kindly old man smiled and said in his funny accent, "I have been in Tzfas with our group. Where have you been?"

"I don't know how to tell you what happened," Eli said. "At my Bar Mitzvah. It was unbelievable. I—uh—I saw Saba. He spoke to me. People think I was crazy or hallucinating or something, but I know it was true, and I guess I just wanted to see you, to tell you, because — I thought you would understand."

The old man reached up to Eli's cheek and gently brushed it with the back of his fingers. He spoke with a brilliant sparkle in his eyes, "Of course I know. I was there! God blessed you. I saw him too, although not like you. I felt him. You are not crazy. Since 1967, when we got back the Kotel, I have never seen a Bar Mitzvah like this one. Never! You should be happy every day the rest of your life!"

Eli nodded, agreeing with him, feeling happy to have found him.

Just then Eli's father came out of the crowd and Eli introduced him to the rabbi.

"You have a very special son, Mr. Bloome," the man said. "I knew his grandfather and if he is one-tenth of that man, he will be a great man too someday, with the help of God..."

Chapter 29

# Doubters and Skeptics

Although Eli loved Israel and felt his future was some-how bound to the country where he was born, he was glad to be home and back to a regular routine.

But then, a day after his return, he had met some friends and made the mistake of telling them about some of the adventures that had happened to him in Israel. He had expected they would be over-awed, as he had been, but they looked at him as if he were crazy.

"A sorcerer? a treasure? an earthquake?" they ech-oed, as Eli listed each experience. "You expect us to believe that? Come on," they had scoffed and turned away. Eli felt ashamed he had said anything.

"If you met my grandfather, you wouldn't say that," he countered. They just laughed.

"You want to see my tefillin?" he said. "They're al-most 200 years old."

"Yeah, right," said the leader of the gang, a 15-year-old named Barry Berman. "That doesn't prove you were held hostage in the house of some Arab sorcerer. Or that you found a treasure and were buried in an earthquake. You think we're stupid? You're just trying to impress us. You probably read some comic book—"

"Okay," said Eli, simmering with indignation, "Would you believe me if I showed you my grandfather's will, written on parchment?"

"No," said Barry flatly. "A will is just a document. Anyone can write one."

"So you think I'm crazy?" Eli said. "You'll see."

"How? You going to make some kind of magic potion and conjure up a curse on my bones?"

The others laughed.

Eli smiled, remembering the flower Saba had crushed in his coat pocket. "Wait and see," he said.

He went home and flew down the basement stairs to where the crate which contained Saba's private belongings had been put in storage. He dug through the crate until he found the green coat Saba had worn in Jaktabar's house. He very carefully spread a white paper on the top of the crate, then turned the coat pocket inside out above the paper. Along with dust and lint and a few cracker crumbs, a considerable amount of golden powder floated onto the paper.

Eli remembered that night in the room of Jaktabar's house. The lights had been off and Eli had not seen the powder Saba had handed him. Likewise, downstairs, where he had sprinkled the powder into the hookah pipe, it had also been too dark to see its actual color. But looking at it closely in the light of the cellar, he felt certain it was the remains of the special flower that Saba had used against Jaktabar and his men.

He thought a long time. He certainly did not want to use the powder against his friends. Even if they accused him of making up stories, even if they insulted him, he would not use something so dangerous against them.

Eli took a deep breath and sighed. The initial sting from Barry Berman's remarks had worn off. He didn't have to prove anything to anyone. But still...

He lifted up the sides of the paper and sprinkled the powder into a plastic film container. Maybe there would come a time when this magical powder would prove useful, he thought.

You never know.

Chapter 30

# A Final Decision

The next day, Eli was sitting in his mother's car, outside a dress shop where she had gone to have something altered. The film container was in the pocket of his baseball jacket.

Down the sidewalk, he saw Barry Berman approaching with a few others. When Barry saw him, he pointed and laughed and made the witchy sound. Eli felt the anger burning inside him, but he managed to keep it down. He thought of Saba and what he would have done. Nothing, probably. He would have let it go, or maybe he wouldn't have said anything to anyone in the first place. But it was too late for that.

"Here he is, our little witchbuster," Barry sneered from the sidewalk. "Exorcise anybody today, Bloome? Cast any magic spells? Hah-hah-hah," he laughed and the others followed his example.

Eli called back, "Barry, come here." He reached inside his pocket for the container. "You want to see something from my grandfather?"

"Oh boy, what is it, a voodoo doll? Show me."

Eli opened the container. He could not really see inside, but there was enough light to make out the golden powder at the bottom.

"What is it?"

"You remember the story. It's the powder from a flower my grandfather used to turn our kidnappers against each other."

"Right," Barry laughed mockingly. "And I suppose if I take that, I'll grow fangs and attack my baby brother in his crib."

"I don't know what you'd do. That would depend on you."

"Yeah, what does that mean?" Barry was bending in the window of the car. Eli could see the red veins in the whites of his eyes.

"Listen, Barry, you have to understand something very simple. Everything in the world has a spiritual root, a power which gives it life. The power behind this flower makes people violent and jealous."

"Oh yeah, so if I took it—"

"You have to smoke it, I think, that's how they took it."

"They? Oh yeah. So if I took it, it would make me violent and jealous?"

Eli nodded slowly, watching the big 15-year-old. He suddenly felt afraid of what the boy might do.

"So give me some," said Barry, "I'll see if it works at football tryouts tomorrow."

"Here he is, our little witchbuster," Barry sneered from the sidewalk. "Exorcise anybody today, Bloome?"

"I can't take responsibility," said Eli.

"No, I'll take responsibility. Give it to me."

"You don't know what you're doing and besides, you were the one who was calling me a liar and saying I made up everything. How come you suddenly believe?"

"I'll do anything to make starting linebacker."

"Sorry." He put the cap on the container just as his mother was coming out of the shop.

"I'll get back to you, tonight," said Barry. "Don't use it before me. You hear, Bloome? You hear?" He backed away from the car, pointing threateningly, his eyes unflinching.

# Chapter 31
# An Important Message

Eli sat with his legs dangling in the old tree fort. He was staring out through the leaves at the stars. He remembered the last time he had sat there, the night he had read the secret letter.

He glanced at the boarded wall where he had painted, King David's Tower. It seemed so long ago, so innocent and childish, especially now that he had seen the real Tower of King David.

"Bloome, you up there?" he heard Barry Berman's scratchy voice sawing through the night. "Your mother said you were up here. You got the stuff."

"What stuff?" Eli said, looking down at Barry and the gang of kids surrounding him.

"What stuff?! You know. The stuff that's supposed to make me strong enough to blitz any quarterback."

"Oh that," Eli said. "Barry, you really believed me? Com'on, you were right all along. I was just making up the story."

"What?!" Barry exclaimed, the anger heavy in his voice. "After I already took my dad's pipe."

Eli didn't answer. He had decided that these kids were not ready to know about his Saba. Some of them might be older than him in years, but none of them surpassed him in experience. Not where Saba was concerned.

Barry called up the tree, "Bloome, you know something, you are weird. A-1 weird! But who cares. I got my father's pipe. This may be a good time to check it out."

Eli heard the group shuffle away, impressed with Barry's decision to smoke his father's pipe.

Suddenly the phone rang. His mother called from the porch.

"Eli, it's someone from Israel," his mother called from the porch. "He says he met you at the Kotel!"

Eli jumped down from the fort and raced inside.

"Hello...Rabbi?" he said, breathlessly.

"Shalom, Eliyahu," the voice said through the static over the line. "You did the right thing. Everything that happened is between us, yes? Your Saba liked to say, *'Silence is a fence for wisdom.'*"

Eli wondered how the rabbi knew. He didn't know what to say. Sensing his hesitation, the rabbi said, "Do not worry, Eliyahu. You will find the words when the time comes." Then he said goodbye and hung up.

"Who was that, Eli?" his mother called from the porch. "What did he want? It must have been important."

Eli stared out the window into the night. "It was important. An important message," he smiled. "A message from Saba."

Also available from **PITS****ANY**

# THE GANG OF FOUR
## Kung-fooey to the Rescue

by Yaacov Peterseil

# THE GANG OF FOUR
## Nest of the Jerusalem Eagle

by Yaacov Peterseil

# The Secret of the
# Space Scrolls

## and *Cholent*

# Double Dare of the Gooblyglop

## by Tova Guttmann